JAKARTA

JAKARTA

Rodrigo Márquez Tizano

Translated by Thomas Bunstead

COFFEE HOUSE PRESS
Minneapolis
2019

First English-language edition published 2019
Copyright © 2016 by Rodrigo Márquez Tizano
c/o Indent Literary Agency, www.indentagency.com
Translation © 2019 by Thomas Bunstead
Book design by Rachel Holscher
Author photograph © Valentina Siniego Benenati
Translator photograph © Carlotta Luke

First published in Spanish as *Yakarta* in 2016. This edition is under license
from Editorial Sexto Piso, Mexico (www.sextopiso.mx).

Coffee House Press books are available to the trade through our primary distribu-
tor, Consortium Book Sales & Distribution, cbsd.com or (800) 283-3572. For personal orders, catalogs, or other information, write to info@coffeehousepress.org.

Coffee House Press is a nonprofit literary publishing house. Support from private foundations, corporate giving programs, government programs, and generous individuals helps make the publication of our books possible. We gratefully
acknowledge their support in detail in the back of this book.

LIBRARY OF CONGRESS CATALOGING-IN-PUBLICATION DATA

Names: Márquez Tizano, Rodrigo, 1984– author. | Bunstead, Thomas, translator.
Title: Jakarta / Rodrigo Márquez Tizano ; translated by Thomas Bunstead.
Other titles: Yakarta. English
Description: First English-language edition. | Minneapolis : Coffee House
    Press, 2019.
Identifiers: LCCN 2018060440 (print) | LCCN 2018061648 (ebook) | ISBN
    9781566895712 (ebook) | ISBN 9781566895637 (trade paper)
Classification: LCC PQ7298.423.A7614 (ebook) | LCC PQ7298.423.A7614
    Y3513 2019 (print) | DDC 863/.7—dc23
LC record available at https://lccn.loc.gov/2018060440

PRINTED IN THE UNITED STATES OF AMERICA

26 25 24 23 22 21 20 19   1 2 3 4 5 6 7 8

For Paula

Thought I heard a dog barking. It's possible. The simplest basic units develop into the richest natural patterns.

DONALD BARTHELME

JAKARTA

1.

I'm going to meet up with the boys. I'm going searching in the tunnels. I have no choice: the stone has spoken. The stone is opaque and smooth to the touch, like the tongues of the dogs we used to find on the way out to Arroyo Muerto. Day after day, Clara sets herself before it, and it responds with a pink, spreading glow, which little by little begins to illuminate the insides of the animals. Clara's forehead becomes a prism, the light expands, and so do the distended beasts. All are alike inside: all are cavernous. The light rises from the surface of the stone in spindling pink tines, usually breaking off in four directions. They are luminous stalactites, they plunge into the four corners of our room, a room with next to nothing in it: a vase, a dog, a couple of coins. On the peeling walls, red and blue flecks of paint. I had a teacher in fifth grade, a nun with a wrinkled face, wrinkles of the kind you only ever see on nuns (or on receipts, I think, or in regions prone to earthquakes). She taught geography—of a sort. Everywhere had been discovered by then, and in the absence of new lands to discuss she would get diverted into talk of the soul. Or, put another way: she would call out countries, and we had to name the capitals. And from there she would start talking about the afterlife, going into long and winding descriptions of what happens to suicides when they get suspended.

2.

All the great poxes, choleras, fevers, and plagues, as with all significant outbreaks of dysentery, tuberculosis, and malaria, have been transmitted by insects. One body decays, another moves in: thus the demolition begins. It's one of the possible paths. A malfunction is all it takes, or, we could perhaps say, an oversight. Once it has begun, there isn't any way to stop it, no turning back. In the first several months the Department of Hygiene, Social Services, and Public Wellbeing insisted rats were to blame, but in fact it was their parasites we humans were susceptible to. True, bitches carrying the disease turned aggressive, began biting the ankles of unsuspecting strangers. And their original victims were children—that, too, is true. The hours they spent playing down at the foreshore made them easy targets: they chased vermin, they rooted around in mounds of trash and beer crates, under rocks. On our long reconnaissance hikes, in radio contact with HQ throughout, we began to come across dozens of child cadavers littering the shore: lodged between boulders or half buried in the sands, and all of them stinking to high heaven. They took less time than the rats to die and less still to decompose. I could not stop thinking of all the similarities— from a certain distance, and with my senses perhaps dulled by the hazmat suit, plus the warping effect of panic—between these carcasses and those of the roadkill dogs I used to go out gathering with my schoolmates. Morgan would check for a pulse and stick to filling in the forms. I wrote on labels in marker, attaching them to the big toes, or, if they no longer had big toes, to the least ill-preserved extremities. Sometimes the job was that of a gravedigger: drear mechanics in hi-vis hazmat suits. A shit job, the salary a pittance, less! All of which did nothing to prevent us from carrying out our duties with the indolence common to all subalterns, natural to all of those to whom the shit jobs fall. Nor were we authorized to pick up the bodies: as soon as we spotted them, we were just to radio back. The guys taking the calls would then fill out further reams of paperwork, complete with sections, subsections, and fields concerning a panoply of specifications, some technical, others not so technical, but all necessary before the Ministry of Public Affairs would agree to send an inspection team. Once one of their experts had come and confirmed the Ź-Bug and not, say, a common cold as cause of death, we were authorized to call the Civil Registrar, who in turn sent an ambulance to transport the body to the labs. This was the method we piloted. Would it have been more effective to comb the foreshore, just filling up crates with bodies? Maybe at the start. But some kind of order had to be imposed, even among those mountains of garbage and meat. Without order, survival becomes a tricky business indeed. In those early days, another group of operatives was subcontracted, more as a precaution than out of any worry about the amount of overtime we were doing. Some parents, fearing the worst, handed over their offsprings' passwords in advance, while others, perhaps not the parents but their neighbors, jammed the phone lines to complain about the unbearable stench given off by other people's children—a reek comparable only to that of the tidal marshes in high summer. But the phone calls soon abated, the army evacuated the city, and we went down into the tunnels. Then we were given some respect—either that or written off as godforsaken, beyond saving, no hope for us apart from that of being struck down by the Ź-Bug. Thus it began, if begin it ever did: we entered the earth, and the disease was left to self-propagate in silence. The parasites came from within, lapping at the infected rat until its insides turned liquid, collapsing those furred little cadavers before going off in search of other rats, or men.

3.

The ball strikes very slightly over the line: out of bounds. A few inches at most, but I know. No need for a replay. Over the years these things become second nature. The scorching trajectory of the ball is very clear to me, and the speedometer nestled in the lower corner of my screen reads 745 kilometers per hour. After a play made up of twelve straight shots and twenty carambolas (side wall > front wall > floor), the red team is announced the winner. An outcome nobody expected, least of all the red team, only recently promoted to the first division and generally seen as tending to wilt in the final third. It would have been the easiest thing in the world to drop the ball short, a little feather shot, forcing the opposition to break formation and come to the front of the Vakapý court to return it. But instead, a rocket of a shot came in from the red forward's ahaka, and though the Yagwatý blues may have been able to guess where the ball would wind up, or at least the forward's intention when he swiveled his body and planted his standing leg at a forty-five-degree angle, my opponent wasn't. So he presses CHALLENGE, calling for the replay: the sequence, featuring Player#56148, comes buzzing down the line from the Upper Curumbý Data Center. The bookmaker hub signs off on the request, and within a fraction of a second we're seeing all the available angles at a variety of different playback speeds. And it was, indeed, above the luminous strip that marks out-of-bounds on the front wall, though by a bare two millimeters: a UV test is ordered simultaneously, they switch the lights, and you can clearly see where the ball (daubed as always in UV paint) left a mark. Then the match stats flash up, cascading in no apparent order down the right-hand side of the screen. Beneath that is my account, constantly going up and down according to the slew of simultaneous bets I've got on different facets of different games happening in all the different stadia. With this miss, a little bump in my Credits. I'm holding my own, at least, if not exactly sweeping the board; this small triumph is more a stay of execution than anything, postponing the inevitable defeat. Any time you're deep in the Vakapý (which is every time you play), it's like a rope is coiled around your neck, and the deeper you go, the tighter the rope becomes, tighter and tighter until there's nothing for it but to get up and walk across that taut strip: dire straits. And that's exactly where I find myself, may as well give it a go. Grandma's advice to my brothers and me was always to economize our efforts by looking at only the stats from the last twenty matches. After all, she pointed out, though the life expectancy of the players varies from developer to developer, they rarely last more than thirty matches, and that's in a pinch—they need to get on a winning streak pretty quick, otherwise they just get junked, stripped, parts reused. She was right, at least on the mechanics side of things: in those days it was all two-stroke carburetors rather than the multipoint fuel-injection systems we now see, or the øilsteâm currently used for calibration. Nowadays any player with a decent set of implants, plus regular servicing of course, can go for ten years plus. All of which aside, the numbers are and always have been king, regardless of the quality of the kit. Grandma herself was constantly saying as much. It goes without saying that when she died she was heavily in debt to the Department of Chaos and Gaming. Since then, a percentage of anything I earn has gone toward paying off each of Grandma's disastrous calls.

4.

Clara stands before the stone; I watch. She has sleep in her eyes, thick, pasty gobs of it all around her eyes, in fact. The next thing to come into focus is a fan, slowly revolving above our heads, churning the warm air in the room. *Tick . . . tick . . . tick.* The vase on the table, the coins scattered around it, the superimposed, semitransparent dog. But it is the stone that draws the eye. It's well known that rheum crystallizes more quickly the farther it spreads from the tear duct. So chemistry dictates. Dust, dead skin cells: these things we slough off, and rarely does the process happen in reverse. Once we're up and running, the business of the day underway, we don't really think about it. This ocular rheum expels things the body refuses. Studies have been carried out to establish a link between sleep cycles and the body's secretions at night, but there's been little success in divining the content of dreams on the basis of these apparent physical concomitants. Sometimes it takes hours for the rheum to be wiped off, for any number of reasons—embarrassment, negligence, lack of hygiene. Helguera used to keep a collection of these crusty-sticky gobbets beneath his desk. They came in all shapes and sizes, a suspended catalog of dark, hardened scree. Birdface Helguera and his stalactite collection. Tiny Zermeño and his repertoire of naked bodies. Morgan, Morgan, Morgan: when you joined us together, *what* were you joining together? These are the thoughts playing inside my head. I am but a link in a chain, or the vaguest approximation of a link in a chain: one foot still in dream, and one here, where I watch Clara with the stone. A pulse of light. Another. Clara, utterly drained, bends forward over her skinny knees. She stays like that for a number of minutes before suddenly lifting her head up once more. Again, the images start to form.

5.

Our high school was part of a religious charity responsible for numerous educational institutions—boarding schools as well as high schools—across the state. Apart from giving us an education, the school did work on behalf of those described by our ancient headmistress, with such inimitable sweetness, as the most needy. I once asked Grandma, Needy in what way? Needy for lots of things, she said. Food, clothing, a roof over their heads. Everyone needs something. Even us? *Especially us.* I was struck by the matter-of-factness of her reply, the brusque echo of suddenly finding out: we, too, were poor. Morning after morning, from the moment my alarm went off and throughout my walk past the dockyards to school, I would ruminate over her words, each syllable sonorous but also somehow profane: *Especially us.* Over and over they resounded against the cobbles of the seawall, a soft, sibilant rumble, mixing with the *slap slap* of my sandals all the way from the weather vane and past the little crowd of hollow-cheeked bums straining to hear the tinny Vakapý reports or talk show reruns on a miniscule radio, clutching themselves for warmth, cowering together as though bound for the slaughterhouse, gazing out to sea, out at the pier with plants inching through the cracks, plants of every color, like some kind of reflection of the people of this land, spurts of unruly sargassum flattened by salt and wind and having never needed any invitation to come and settle along this coast—but none of that really registered, my mind so entirely consumed by Grandma's unexplained and yet conclusive words that I could think of nothing else, until sure enough my path took me into the schoolyard, past the tetherball posts, past heads slick with hair gel and, as a wave of antiseptic-soap smell washed over me, into the mildewed school building, a great ramshackle edifice that some upright priest and his acolytes had filled with abacuses, desks, many wastepaper baskets, benches, paddles for doling out reprimands, more desks, all child-sized and vandalized with a combination of child-safe scissors, compasses, and felt-tip pen: messages, threats, nicknames, declarations of love, declarations of hate, equations, defunct or foreign systems of measurement, all also countless, all overlapping and obscuring but simultaneously underscoring one another, and further messages, and further equations, desks upon desks and children upon children, until eventually, in the fullness of time, this agglomeration came to be known by the name of the school. A school full of the needy. On it went in my thoughts: thoughts of why only some people are defined thus when, without exception, everyone is composed of needs, we are all utterly and completely at the mercy of our needs, and there is nothing to be gained from isolating or singling any of them out, far from it, in fact, each need is integrated into society's very warp and weft, to the point that society can even be thought of as little more than a network of ramified needs, distributed and organized in the same way skeletal or muscular networks are distributed and organized; consider (I considered) the fact that parts of the skeleton and parts of the muscular complex *may be* independently distinguishable as objects of anatomical study, according to the function of each, the areas they occupy, their greater or lesser subcutaneous depth, plus whatever tissues comprise them—all true—but they justify their existence only in the *overall* functioning of the body: well, the same surely goes for this or that particular need, want, or desire. They aren't caused by other *people,* and still less by any *thing,* being anterior to our species, as well, therefore, to the effects that accompany our existence. Such needs have the capacity to render one another void, and may, at any moment, even if recently acquired, work against and ultimately displace those formerly assumed to be the only, ultimate, essential needs. The nuns, meanwhile, themselves arranged according to height and complexion, watched us line up along the patio also according to stature, raising their battered hurricane lamps to inspect the length of our hair, the sewing jobs done on buttons, the shine of any shoes we may be lucky enough to have on our feet, always checking our appearances before matins—like carrion birds that, long before they do anything about the visible portion of their own needs, are able to calculate the remaining life in the unfortunate creatures they will in due course devour.

6.

This city has two great enemies: Vakapý, and the industry that surrounds it. It is largely accepted that the two are synonymous, that they spring from the same source and are in every practical sense indivisible, and that it would therefore be ridiculous to understand them as distinct, even when the alliance owes more to pure chance than any real balance between performance, results, and profits. Some predicted a loss of interest when the Department of Chaos and Gaming forced the main teams, the very wealthy and money-spinning ones, to switch their centers of operation to the capital in a difficult-to-argue-with effort to "regularize the tax situation and sweep away the gangsterism that has sullied popular culture and the intangible heritage of our nation." The result turned out to be quite the opposite: removing the money from those far-flung betting hives cut out whole swathes of middle men, making it easier to bypass the tariffs (sometimes just kickbacks) imposed by the government and their enforcers, and easier, therefore, to go on squandering our well-earned Credits. Which is simply to say that the money, which we were bound to lose anyway, began to be lost in a more organized way.

7.

Clara sometimes asks about my time in the Ź-Brigade, questioning
both dosages and methodology. She poses the question and then
gazes off at nothing, at the stone, down at her belly. She glances past
me as though I'm not there, or as though in fact I'm nothing but a
reflection of myself, or some glimmering, guttering series of images.
I know the emptiness is something else. Muscle, cartilage, phlegm,
blood. Something that fills us at times, without our ever belonging to it, and certainly without it ever belonging to us. That which
rots when the body ceases to function. And then I search around
in my pockets and come up with four pieces of metal, which makes
six altogether if we add them to the two on the table, the ones next
to the Chinese vase that may not in fact be Chinese (no dragons
on it, no golden cats, not even any ideograms that would qualify it
as Chinese), right, it may not be, except that everything's made in
China nowadays, so very likely the vase was too. On the vase, a dog.
Or, rather: one is unthinkable lest the image of the other overlaps it.
Everything depends on something else, says Clara, rolling her head
in slow circles. And in turn, on something else.

8.

Anyone who's ever set foot in a Vakapý stadium knows that what
the fans really get off on are the stats. The implications and ruptures,
the chance to give yourself entirely to unpredictability, to pour body
and mind into an order composed of unforeseeable confluences and
divergences; moves, plays, stats. So here it is, dearest larvae of mine:
the Vakapý stadium as such no longer exists, but Vakapý will never
die. It'll outlive us all, just like the Bug. It was around long before
us and will be around long after we're gone. Money has a similarly
never-ending quality, an immortal aspect even, in its deferred promises: so sweet, and at the same time so dissonant. That was certainly

how it sounded on the track that separated the stands from the court, across which the crowd roared out their speculations, bandying about sums that would never become the reality of cash in their pockets but that reverberated off the court's trio of walls regardless, over the heads of the multitude, over the mantle of smoke that lay above their heads, over crumpled slips and cocktails held aloft. Thus money: little more than a knock-on effect, a necessary evil in adding extra spice to the vices associated with unforeseeable chance. The ultimate explanation for Vakapý's astonishing and long-lasting appeal lies in random probability distributions and patterns that, for all their (considerable) susceptibility to statistical analysis, can never be foretold with any precision. Though different both in nature and provenance, the players and the gamblers have become fully interdependent, the upshot being a kind of resistance to that irremediable, wearisome will to improve, the throat-gnawing need to always get better in some way. *Progress* is a word much used in Atlantika, and its presence in our motto and on the town crest is no coincidence. It undergirds bridges, rivers, and ports, even the seas, just as it runs through sermons and so many elegant speeches, lends its neat little trochee to the ancestral rite of the inauguration of public works, because men of vision know to align themselves with the certainty evinced by *progress,* by godsends, Credits from heaven, and the kind of blessings we are obviously due, rather than with the mean past, which, by dint of being the past—or having taken place under another administration—no one wants to think about anymore: to lay that foundation stone with one eye on the horizon, to cut the inaugural ribbon like a person cleaving two worlds, to pose for the photo with all the glad-ragged VIPs and their Botoxed ladies who will occupy the tabloid pages for days on end, nobody bothering to mention that the cement was shoddily laid, roof joists were loose, the sleepers and steel frames used for wing x of pavilion y were little more than figments of some con man's imagination, or that the cardiology team was still waiting at the border for the work permits to come through, or that—never mind, I hereby announce, fellow citizens, with heart and mind fixed unerringly on the tremendous service these facilities will provide for generations to come, as I unveil the all-new Hospital of Progress, the unprecedented Progress Avenue, the state-of-the-art Progress Boulevard, the highly progressive Progress Quarter. And flash go all the cameras. Progress also, of course, figures prominently in the deed poll as one of our most popular male names. After Juan, Progress is the most popular name for boys. Truly, truly, this is the land of Vakapý and all its attendant wretchedness. And don't just take my word for it: ask the first person you meet in the street around here (chances are he'll answer to Juan Progreso Pérez). He'll back me up: Vakapý first, worry about dinner later. Thus has it always been: even in times of famine or plague, even when the Ź-Bug was at its most virulent, never would a weekend pass without all the Vakapý stadia along the coast, from Las Huertas to San Martín Jagua, full to the rafters. Each of the principal cities had its own team, comprised of the galaxy of journeyman foreign players who were always the main attraction. Inside the stadium things worked differently: when a match merited it, whether because the players were superstars or rivalries were sufficiently intense, entire towns would mobilize, traveling in rented buses or in great processions of smaller vehicles, clogging all B-roads and earthen tracks as yet unfamiliar with the technology of cobblestones, so the pride of these far-flung places made its way to the stadium in question, the scene of the showdown, no matter the distance, no matter the cost. They say it's about identity. The world being what it now is, though, identity is just about the last thing your average gambler cares about. Or they care about it if they can use it in the game as part of a double bluff. The only thing left to identify with is the numbers. In spite of everything, the odd illegal field still exists, in remote corners of the country, listing into the sea in some cases, all of them out of reach of league officials. Low-level betting takes place in these semiderelict locales, nothing more than loose change—a question, more than anything, of some people not wanting the game's beginnings to be forgotten altogether. And even in the beginning it was very clear: what goes up must come down, and sooner or later everyone loses. That is the game, that is its defining contour: an arc. And that is not progress. Anyone who says they play to win only feeds the beast, the incontestable nature of which is loss.

9.

I remember starting back to school one year after the winter vacation. The stone remembers it too. During vacation one of the novices hanged herself in the school chapel. We heard about it through Zermeño: Zermeño had a little business stealing copies of the local newspaper from his father's barbershop and then selling the Page Threes to other children at recess. His own little racket. Everyone had one. Mine consisted of making myself as inconspicuous as the cracks in the walls, whereas Zermeño peddled previously perused pornography, an unintended consequence of which was that we were sometimes apprised of happenings in the world. The paper in question was printed on stock so cheap that when you held it up to the light the words, classifieds, and nude females on either side would intermingle. For my part, Mondays meant handing over most of the money I'd stolen out of Grandma's purse during the weekend. In exchange I got the results from all the games and the player trading cards that usually came with the Sunday paper. I remember it well: it was the start of a new year but the end of the holidays, that difficult contradiction to which we gradually had to become accustomed. The bell had barely gone for the first lesson of term, Zermeño took out the paper with the article about the novice's suicide, and a knot of children gathered. The article was one of the many that told of the near-daily hangings in Atlantika; at a time before the Ź-Bug came, and for want of anything exciting to relate, these always occupied column inch after column inch. Suicides, obituaries, and the weather on the Atlantik seaboard: therein the pith and marrow of our new journalism. Zermeño gave a hurried, nasal reading to the gathered kids, but there wasn't a picture of the young woman's corpse. The article did have a picture of the chapel exterior, a black mourning ribbon over the entrance, the school crest, the traffic posts along the pavement, a policeman smoking his fourth cigarette of the morning—but not the novice, not even the coffin. The photo would have been taken early one Saturday morning, or just before midday. It always seemed strange to me that the photographer didn't bother getting a close-up of the body. It doesn't take a genius to realize that we readers prefer a corpse over stones every time.

10.

The Bug. Â, B, Ć, and so on: every twenty or thirty years, it comes back. At times it stays away for as long as half a century, at others, outbreaks occur every half decade. It takes many, many different forms, which is why in this city it has never been properly dealt with. There's just one thing we know for sure: our destiny is not to be avoided. And, it should also be understood, it is a destiny not so much concerned with damaging us as with leaving us utterly confounded. The stone sucks the light from the room. In the last few days its behavior has changed, throbbing with a deep blackish light that seems to signal a new life brewing inside it. The nun would have come up with all manner of names for such an entity: spirit, substance, essence, psyche, psyches, awareness, sensation, will, intelligence, imagination, memory, conscience, comprehension, understanding, inner life. I believe it is anything but: it's the dregs, the overspill; it's all that nobody wants. Clara doesn't believe in those kinds of superstitions either. But she now suspects that, if the stone did come into existence with such an intangible, fragile entity inside it, it isn't there anymore. If it had any physical reality, and could therefore have been made available to buy or sell on some kind of market, someone would have acquired it long ago. Now she thinks she's found something: the first discovery to suggest all the effort has been worth it. I agree but say nothing. She, however, along with the stone, seems convinced. The true treasures, she says, are never things you look for; either they come to you or they don't, or maybe you convince yourself that they're going to come and then a day arrives when you happen upon a jewelry box or a sepia scroll marked with a cross: a signal, or something you at least take as a signal, that allows you to dream of better times, better climes, only eventually, after so long at the bottom of the pile, to end up feeling it's better to give up all hope, to come round to loss as your standard setting, to believe that the treasure will arrive only by sheer fluke and at a time of its choosing, which in turn means that it, as well as any hope for it, must be securely stowed away, for it is ultimately easier to take responsibility for one's own frustration, to become accustomed to the frustration, or at least to deal with it in the same way you might deal with some known quantity (like the metric system, like an electricity transformer), than to let yourself be trampled by certainty, the utter crushing certainty that there's nothing inside the box apart from nothing—a million tiny bits of nothing. Anything but that. And Clara—dear Clara—is nearly nothing, for all that she may still be in one piece—just about. How battered her body looks. Surely she can't go on much longer. She bares her teeth, and not in a smile: and what teeth, so white, so even! They are all the more eye-catching given the weight she's lost. The little that remains of her emaciated arms seems but one more facet in the inventory of objects in the room: stone, bra, vase, dog, flesh, coins. All present and correct. Time, or the sequence of intervals otherwise known as time, is no longer of much use to her: for her, all time is deposited in the stone. My time and her own. Has the stone grown over the course of the days? Clara has been shrinking, that much is clear, and in comparing the two of them it is possible to say, Yes: there's no way she can go on much longer, her abandonment to the mineral world is well advanced, whereas the stone is like a bouncing child of about three. Aside from the stone, all that remains of Clara is her hunger. The blotches on her hands; the dull, lusterless hair; the odd string of saliva at the corner of her mouth. It is today:

she does not say this in words, simply shakes her head. We use words now only for things that aren't truly urgent.

11.

The government trotted out the line, "Vakapý: a tradition of innovation." According to this mantra, endorsed by those for whom Vakapý, betting, and all denizens of Atlantika comprise a fundamental trinity, our town is the very crucible for the clash—and eventual fusion—of three strands of Vakapý history: the Vakapý of the natives, who long before the arrival of the first settlers were playing a kind of ritualistic hipball (the ball itself usually a shrunken human head, by and large that of some vanquished foe, placed inside rubber casing, and the aim being to shoot it through the seven side-on hoops in the walled temple-cum-stadium); the Albýno Vakapý, an underground version in which the players had to roll their balls along a sloping sidewall on the way to hitting a jack; and finally, that of the invaders, which, with its use of paddles and curved, wicker basket-gloves (not so dissimilar to our modern-day ahaka), has roots most clearly in the leisure pursuits of Numidian tribes. The rules, ways of winning, and materials, the use or otherwise of a wall or a slope, are, however, secondary in importance. In these pastimes, as with any of the ways in which we choose to squander our time on planet earth, the important thing is and has always been the chance to win money in wagers.

12.

Morgan spoke not a single word for a long time—six weeks, two months. A sadness that had knocked him sideways. Nor was this just his usual crestfallen attitude to the world, far from it. Not the crooked, yellow teeth; not the distinctive sound he used to make when sucking his bifurcate tongue against his palate, the click that disguised and revealed his spleen—I don't mean these things, but another kind of silence, one issuing out of some faraway place, a future-contaminated place, verging on the adult. A solid silence, corpulent even, with physical qualities and a tenor that varied according to the distribution of the desks: sometimes all it took was being seated near Morgan to feel that desolate charge, more akin to the disfiguring effects gravity can have on certain materials, like us, or like a colony of rats or mound of trash—anything at all—than to the absence of sound. It was, I am certain, a form of resistance. Of quelling the outside noise. Out of all our classes, an hour of national history was the best bet for disappearing completely. Our teacher, a grizzled priest, miser, and drinker rolled into one, always came in reeking of pastis. The few words he deigned to speak in class tended to come out as grunts. He had a fishhook for a right hand. Morgan claimed he sustained the injury in the War of 910, long before any of us was born, during a brutal crackdown on the Faith: all icons and scriptures, anything deemed to play a part in fomenting it, were destroyed. The temples were closed down, and the ensuing, all-encompassing dust cloud swallowed every single chalice, cincture, and hunk of consecrated bread in the land. In spite of the danger, men of faith flocked to town squares to be blessed by priests who went around disguised as agave farmers. Precisely one month after the initial order had been given, new ones were issued, and by the time the sun came up next morning, the renegade priests had all been relieved of a limb. It went down as the Night of the One-Handed Cocoons and was the start of a little over a decade of hostilities between army and church. Thousands upon thousands died. Any time Grandma drank (cognac her poison), she'd weep and tell us of the terrible atrocities committed: how the Spawn Tanks were shut down, too, how you'd come across dead soldiers in fields on a daily basis, how blood flowed through the streets, not to mention the sharp increase in infections; the young larvae were hidden away in basements to learn the catechism by the light of a few votive candles, but the true light continued to illuminate them: our radiant Lady of the Chrysalids. The youngsters studied scripture and memorized the Canticle of the Caterpillar; our Recuźant great great-grandparents ferried the priests to these underground prayer rooms like contraband, risking their lives in the process, but what kind of life would it be anyway, one's soul in perpetual darkness? A soul that never transforms, never emerges from its cocoon, a dormant, untapped soul. In order that life could at least be a project of self-liberation, and though people had to hide away like poachers and night thieves, instruction in the arts of the Spirit continued. Just like in the olden days, when the true faith could be proclaimed only in the Katacombz. The novices hurried to enter the Order of the Lepidoptz, becoming the Padres who went out to preach in the moonlit agave fields with guns at their hips. Their fervor was great, and they defended the faith with all the dignity of true believers: they'd sooner fall with pupae spilling from their fists than forsake the chance to inculcate. The maimed priests were later dubbed the Martyrs of Saint Źirconium, though their elevation was, and still is, a matter of some controversy. Sometimes I wonder how utterly rotten Grandma would feel if she could see how the ranks of the Magnetiźed have swelled, glorified ragpickers shuffling around in their maize-colored shawls, rooting for scrap metal with their long grabbers and clanking metal detectors. Logically enough, for the priest who taught our history lessons—Fish Hook to us—military discipline and religious formation went hand in hand. Just as unsurprising was the inability of any of our teachers to quell talk of the novice who hanged herself. The week began—as every week did—with readings from the Settlerz Scripture. But the ancient nun, ringing the bell at the end of recess, and without bothering to consult the parent body, felt the need to do something about the images that had been incubating in our minds over the winter, that conflagration fueled by the holidays and tabloid newspapers.

13.

It's important to follow instructions. Sometimes the numbers freeze momentarily, but if you disconnect without first hitting PAUSE, there's a chance they'll stay planted in front of your retina for hours, or even days. Static statistics, numb numbers, signifying the square root of nothing—like the old clocks outside the Brigade barracks or the unmoving chrome timepieces on the refinery ovens at the mill. Visual details of the Vakapý matches that are incredibly hard to shake, or fragments of visual details: the floorboards, the baskets, marks left by the ball, bits of bodies. I sometimes wonder whether this residual mosaic is generated on the basis of any predetermined order, some glitch in the memory that nonetheless obeys certain laws, or whether it's purely random. Each gambler has a dedicated drone-camera in the stadium that they personally control; obviously the shots you choose give a sense of your personal take on the game, what aspects you set store by, and even your conception of space itself. You will also never be presented with any images you did not previously select from among the thousands comprising the match—for all that such a selection may have been unconscious. But even so, among the many different things that may cause the Sýstem to freeze, only a few very specific ones will get stuck like this, will really refuse to budge. Take today: the last shot I saw was of a portion of one of the plaýers' arms, possibly the hydraulic elbow, as the final point of the match was being played. It was a Super Close Up, everything in Hyperdetail™, and the ball was just on the verge of being slung out of the midfielder's ahaka, so it looked ever so slightly squashed. I remember, or seem to remember, the play in question: the position of the plaýer's knee in respect to the rest of his body, the V-formation of his team around him. The stoop to gather the ball, the hurling of the ball back at the wall. So why an elbow? Maybe I focus on that only now because the image has stuck inside my vision, because it happens to be within reach—maybe all it's really good for is dazzling my sight and dragging my memory down alleys just as blind. I have also at times imagined, due to the similarities between so many of the images you see in Playback, that the games and the ways in which the gamblers can participate—the two indispensable, interdependent pillars of Vakapý—are the slightest variations on one single, far, far longer game, a game previously watched from a variety of different angles, and that if it has any point, it's the fueling of a process of infinite recreation. I think this, and a second later forget it. I forget it because I have to remember it—fleetingly—the next time I connect. The floating images gradually dissipate, breaking up into less nuanced blocks and lines, then simply a succession of dots, and I eventually feel the ciliary muscles loosen and, finally, am able to blink. The audio takes longer to fall in line with itself: I hear faint voices, the murmurs from the other gamblers. They're going absolutely nowhere, my gambler brethren. In spite of government recommendations, the average session goes on for 336 hours. (I imagine the poor bastard who had to do the counting started to feel pretty sorry for himself at about hour 14.) A crypt-like darkness comes down, obscuring the passageway in which I find myself, while another out-of-kilter frequency comes trickling in: the rebounds, the sound of the players' footfalls as they dash this way and that across the synthetic wood boards of the court, the time-out advertisements, the unmistakable jingle of the Department of Chaos and Gaming. Then I know it'll be only a few minutes before the world rights itself again.

14.

She never mentioned the novice, but then again she didn't need to. She said: Jakarta. And we replied: Indonesia. This was a way of giving the rest of the syllabus short shrift, but there were other consequences: we were divested of our names, for a start, and eased into—in a way, reconciled with—the disappointment of knowing there was a world out there, a fully fledged outside reality, but the only contact we were ever going to have with it was this call-and-response memory game concerning its national jurisdictions and capital cities. It's good to know nice and early if you're going to amount to fuck all. Doubly so to be under no illusions: truly, this is all you're good for. The best thing is to really understand, really and truly: your own innate mediocrity is something you will never overcome. The only danger is to fling yourself over the precipice into what some choose to call hopefulness, others, enthusiasm. There was nothing to distinguish our fourth-grade studies from a politics of pure despair: any enthusiasm we encountered, any upbeat individual, we learned to shun as though it were the Ź-Bug incarnate. And yet the school harbored one dangerous agent of magical thinking: our carpentry teacher. He drifted around the workshop inspecting our work, smiling indulgently at our efforts. Any bit of sanding, chiseling, or sawing, anything at all, no matter how cack-handed, and he'd clap his hands and do a little jig: You've got talent, he would lie. It'd be a tragedy to let it go to waste. Double lie. The job you're learning in here is worthy of respect, a way of being somebody in the world. Double, quadruple, endless lies. Know what Saint Lacewing's father did for a job? Can anybody guess? Another jig. A chill ran down my spine at the sight of his dismal capering, while the boy next to me at the workbench, Fatty Muñoz—pure unleavened mass, all jowls and threadbare clothing—watched me blanch to the point of transparency, though he didn't dare say a word either. I looked at him in turn. How ridiculous he appeared in those moments, how deflated, just like everyone else in class: recoiling but also visibly shrinking, even him seeming somewhat diminished—as though slipping away through the black hole of childhood, into which everything subsides from time to time. Poor Fatty M., his big, benumbed ass, his chubby, useless hands gripping tools he would never wield with anything but utmost ineptitude. In my mind our carpentry teacher was worthy of all the contempt you could muster, the lowest of any low-life I'd ever encountered, certainly the most cruel: there was nothing to be gained by praising Fatty M. like this, letting him suspect he might one day be somebody when the opposite was true; the only thing he was ever going to become was a fuckup—a fucking fiasco of a fuckup, a fat one at that—and then what was our inspirational worker of wood going to do? I'll tell you what: shrug, and assure Fatty Fuckup Muñoz that it was his fault alone he hadn't realized his colossal potential. It's no good having all the right ingredients—which you did, kid, you surely did—if you don't then follow the instructions. Meanwhile the air grew increasingly stale in that cramped workshop, more a shed than anything, barely enough oxygen to go round. There we sat, protective goggles, overalls, planes gripped in faithful hands, gouges, hammers, chisels, wood saws of many kinds, triangles—and that piece of wood in the vice, the one that had been there since the beginning of time, trapped between the rusty jaws, pinned there eons before with dark, labyrinthine rings. My thoughts would drift away to the game, to the Vakapý players cutting elegant diagonals across the court. To loveliest Zulaýma. To really going far—away. Images that alleviated the cramped, clamped sensations. Go on, son, keep on sawing. That's it, nice and steady now. Do it like you're *singing* to the wood. Hear that? Hear the way it sings back? Who's to say, one day they could be naming streets after you.

15.

I pick my way through the morass of cables and gaming stations, latter begetting former. Vestiges of the last game still hang pixel-like in my vision and echo disconcertingly in my ears. The identikit stations are like cramped cubbyholes, no bigger than the antique postage stamps from before the most recent Bug, or even the really tiny ones from the epidemic before that: no ventilation, barely space to breathe, though as I come past I am able to make out the labored or agitated breathing of gamblers of all different physical conditions and ages (so much for the official under-fourteen ban) keeping time with the constantly updated personalized betting offers. There, ensconced in headsets, they see themselves as exceptionally well qualified to judge the odds, deeply versed, measured in all that they do, dons among mere fans, when plainly they're the same scum as the rest of us, parasites supping on Vakapý for anything resembling a thrill, needles dangling from forearms. It's a pretty disgusting exercise: I have to clamber directly over some of them, and my hands and legs become coated in their slather. I have to find my way out somehow and mustn't so much as look at those headsets, *must* avoid getting sucked back into the Vakapý maze once more. Another of the gamblers calls out his disconnect balance, trying to get away—he's into hour twenty-five—but something keeps him there, stuck in the limbo, forever nearly about to win. I carefully pick my way through them, forcing myself not to stop, orienting myself by the huddled, panting bodies. I don't know what's got them so excited—a sudden bump in the Credit allocation, perhaps, or some botched attempt to keep the ball in play, both of which, after all, could be ways of describing life itself, or survival at least. I keep my eye on the halogen bulb beyond the door grate at the far end, light that marks a kind of outer limit to this zone. I push my way to the exit and just before I go out cast a final glance back across at my allies in idleness. I feel for them, I really do.

16.

When the Department of Hygiene, Social Services, and Public Wellbeing announced that the quarantine was over, we were lost. We handed in the hazmat suits, and in exchange, they gave us a city that wasn't ours. The roads began teeming with vehicles and people once more, and it was all downhill from there. Immigrants took the place of the dead, and those who had survived the ravages of the Ź-Bug went and signed on for the paltry welfare stamps again. And back to life creaked the city, its many moving parts: the old ladies back to the bingo halls, the gamblers to their gaming stations, the rapists to the public parks; all the highways and byways were reopened, along with the churches and the whorehouses; and you could get all essential household items in the supermarkets once more (at three times the former price). But the newly established order had no place for us. We left the Ź-Brigade, but in many ways it did not leave us; the only reason I stopped exterminating rats was because they disappeared. Otherwise I imagine I'd have stayed underground, eager for Kovac the Albýno's every command. In the end, with nothing better to do, I started hanging around down at the docks. Then Clara appeared.

17.

Any luck? says Señora Albýno#2460, and immediately repeats herself, which means there's no way of avoiding the question: *Any luck?* No luck. Well, there is: the same as ever. But that isn't luck, I think, it's custom, or habit, it's the same old. I see, she says, *I see,* not batting an eyelid as she glances up at my Credit balance on her screen. She goes back to shuffling a stack of the trashy "education" comics on the counter; the counter itself has a green sheet of glass atop it, with a five-directioned crack that has been mended with numerous layers of Scotch tape. This has been Señora Albýno#2460's establishment for as long as I can remember. The walls in the stationary store have grown old, they're mildewed and fissured, but not her. The place is even legitimate: between the retention files, the starved-looking ranks of teddy bears, the drooping helium balloons, and a sparse stock of cellophane, certificates, bookmarks, and various kinds of paper organized by color and thickness, a framed license has pride of place on the back wall, the writing in four different colors, the inspection stamps numerous. I stand and stare at Señora Albýno#2460's hands, which make short work of the comic strips intended to teach our youth about history and social issues, sorting through them hypnotically: a cascade of the brash, reductive illustrations, glimpses of sideburns, sashes, flags, tricornes. To one side of the counter is a bench and sitting on it a man with an aquiline, flaring nose, the hair on top of his head partially shaved and a toupee sown into the skin of his temples. He looks a bit like one of our nation's famous sons to me—an impression supported by the rapier-swift movements of Señora Albýno#2460's hands, her deft and dexterous gesticulations, which seem, like a clairvoyant's, to have conjured this haggard dignitary of our great and noble country, a country always ready to honor misery when it sees it. He's at the front of the queue, a queue that will eventually stretch half the way round the block. Gaming centers are not in short supply: three to every one citizen of voting/gambling age, the latest government numbers suggest. This particular gaming center, for example, is considered one of the upmarket ones, though the state of the walls and ceiling, and of the carpets, never apparently introduced to a vacuum cleaner, suggests otherwise. The man awaits instructions, rubbing the back of his hand against his chin, a stiff and imploring gesture—a result of his condition. The obvious question is why, now that I've disconnected, I'm still hanging around. Señora Albýno#2460 gives him a sidelong squint, followed by a nod. One more nod: that's his signal. The man jumps up, places his ID on the counter, and hurries past as though she doesn't exist. He pulls open the door, goes through, and swings it softly shut behind him. Señora Albýno#2460's sight lingers momentarily on the back of the shop. A thick pair of glasses, the frames imitation tortoiseshell, perch on the squashed protuberance of her nose. She keeps just one eye on the ID; I'm not sure what the other one is looking at. The interruption seems to take an age, and eventually the gaze of her wayward pupil returns to the papers. At the top of the pile is one that reads "Natural Disasters" and features a list of the most significant catastrophes to befall the country in recent times. Señora Albýno#2460 looks at me—half looks at me. I read somewhere that Albýno optic nerves are more knotted than our own, the wiring back there more complicated, and that this, according to the antiabolitionists at least, has something to do with the congenital deceitfulness they attribute to her kind. By which I mean: at the back of most people's heads, the optic nerves reach to the respective opposite side of the brain, whereas in the case of the Albýnos all is an untidy crisscrossing and tangling and even, in places, fusing. The upshot being this ocular drift, plus all the bodily grace of marionettes with broken spindles, though it does also mean they're able to swivel each eye independently, 180 degrees horizontally and 90 degrees up or down. So it goes—none among our academic geniuses, let alone our representatives in parliament, have come anywhere near dispelling prejudices that sprang up almost as soon as the first settlers arrived, bringing the Albýnos with them in shackles. They made pacts with historically oppressed indigenous tribes, which in turn, at the urgings of a monk who had been living among them for some time, agreed to replace the crab eyes with which they traditionally decorated their good-luck charms with Albýno eyes instead; to gods old and new alike, they now began bringing talismans made of pigmentless flesh. Some people still believe that these neural connections, which mean in well-lit places that they can see only a reduced color spectrum, also account for certain behaviors. Strange how something so obvious can be the cause of such disagreement: it's possible to glimpse, through their pinkish retinas, the accumulation of nerves beyond. I stand, stare, picture Señora Albýno#2460 as a complex system of fibers: not an easy fit for the comic-didactic schema laid out in our country. She goes on painstakingly filling in registration forms. Another man comes in off the street, identical to the last guy. He's at the front of the queue now. I ask Señora Albýno#2460 for my ID back. Please, I say. First you gotta do my hair, she says absently—absent as a ghost—*First you gotta do my hair,* and I know she won't take no for an answer, and anyway I can't say no because in the time it takes for me to think how long I'll need to drag a comb through her disgusting locks—quite a long time, not so much dithering as stuck in the headlights of my own growing anguish, my growing unease at being separated from Clara and from the stone—she has produced a comb, plus a couple of hair slides and hair bands for good measure. May as well get on with it: I reach over, starting out with a center part—her hair is so thin it's difficult to hold without it tearing. I picture a diadem extending outward from the center, like a flower composed of nerves, the perfect do, and with this in mind split each half into three subsections, start plaiting a la Roumanian, with sections from either side of the head crossing the center. Seven or eight cross-folds, bringing in sections from occipital and parietal, always folding over-under, always keeping the hair taut as I fold in the different tranches, so much so that strands start coming away in my hands—strands at first, then entire tufts. My hands, my clothes, and all about us on the floor, hair of whitest white, strewn like a lot of straw, like we're in a stable, the problem certainly being my zeal once I've committed to the task, my urge to construct a perfectly knot-free diadem, perfectly limned, a crown of braids in honor of the owner of gaming center #2460, fully accredited by the Department of Chaos and Gaming, who now takes up a small beveled hand mirror, nodding: she likes. Nice, she says, *nice,* and I have to agree: in spite of the missing clumps, I've done an OK job, the finishing touch being the colorful hair ties. She goes on nodding, and the next toupeed gambler comes forward, sets down his ID, hurries past, like we're *both* ghosts! Pulls open the door, goes in, shuts it noiselessly behind him. As for me, I don't even say goodbye: I grab my ID and go outside, brushing the hair from my clothes. Outside, the wind is up, part of the usual din in the street. And I was wrong: the queue reaches all the way along this side of the block, to the corner, past the corner, and snakes away down a side street. It's anybody's guess where it ends.

18.

Then I met her. That could be a beginning too. Like: I was walking along the beach when... Oh, such an artless declarative, but sufficiently discreet as to avoid false hopes! Plus I don't actually remember the details: was it Clara who walked up to me, or the other way round? Plus what does it matter. The first thing was me following her footprints: sunk fairly deep, clean edges. A regular sequence of regular footprints. What I needed now—the only thing I needed—was to set eyes on the feet that had left these marks. They came from the sea, or ended in it. It's clear to me now, looking back, that the true beginning of our stone-quest lay with those footprints in the sand. Within days of finding one another we were doing the usual: killing time, her talking about her, me talking about me, general pointless nattering, sex, walks along the esplanade, visits to the uninhabited local cinema. The authorities had dispatched the Ź-Bug, but there were still Department of Hygiene warnings in force; you were expected to wear masks in public places, and physical contact was a big no-no. In any case Clara never liked to be touched in public, though she did like Westerns. In her view, all the stories ever told, past, present, and future, could be boiled down to the conflict between the land and human will. A single pasture, or a thousand head of livestock: all you needed for narrative conflict, right there. White sombrero versus black sombrero. Even the Bible, she said, was just a question of warring sombreros. Her views were far from ideological, they were based in her own authentic interest, if I can put it like that. She had a way of asking questions, and answering them, that enabled the conversation to flow, that gave it a rhythm, dragging out her vowels and dropping so many consonants that any link between them was all but decimated, leaving each of the syllables effectively autonomous, vying for a foothold as actual parts of speech. She'd say *sombrero* and the *eeeee* would get jammed before it even really emerged, rattling around somewhere in her digestive tract: a trapped vowel, struggling to make it out from the mire of warmish body fluids or sticky cells, snagged perhaps on a secret flap inside some tubular organ or other, there it would stay, right the*eeeee*re, the*eeeee*ro, sombre*eeeee*ro, milled or milling around or ground down or just stuck inside the inner workings of her stomach, or the workings of the formation of her words, before finally, eventually surfacing, crossing the threshold of her palate. Only then did the subsequent syllable get to embark on its journey toward articulation. She and I saw each other under strict conditions but with a certain amount of frequency. And then one day she found the stone. I took them both back to my place, stone and girl, gripped by sudden fears. And for a while thereafter there was no time for Vakapý, or time down at the docks. It was these two and nothing else: my life became an exercise in deciphering what it was that joined them. And then one day the images began. Perfection. I didn't need money because money represented an obstacle in my new task, my new life's work. More than just an inconvenience, money became something utterly not worth going after, given that the more a person makes, the greater one's gains, the more acute the possibility of losing it all becomes, an acuteness that quickly transforms into worry. So I gave up all my winnings as lost, and the only thing I now spent any effort on was establishing whether Clara, in the stillness of her trances, intensely subsumed in the stone visions, was still breathing. On rare occasions when the room became so crammed with the images that it felt like the roof would squash us from above, I slipped out and diluted my brain for a little while with the distraction of some Vakapý. Sometimes I don't even need to see the ball in flight. The sound is enough. Enough just to plug in, hear the welcome jingle, the faintest whiff of a game. You lose yourself in any case. Whatever happens, the Sýstem wins. It's the Sýstem, you see.

19.

Though the city stagnates, and any possible works are safely buried under endless red tape, it's still a place you never fully get a handle on. There is perpetual haze, which the light does little to dissipate: the polluted air and seawater meld to become one single salty airborne solution. That's often how it is at sunrise, and how it stays until sunset—it's often pretty impossible to distinguish the coming or going of that astral body. The wind and the constant metallic clatter of the extractors, day and night, are further disorienting factors, filling heads and chests with the sickly stink of deep-fat fryers and cream cakes. I make my way south down Avenida Almirante Ruíz-Cuevas. It's the longest way home: it takes you down past the docks, you hop onto 14 de Octubre, and that goes all the way to the north side. The docks tend to be deserted at this hour. A group of boys is standing at the railings—on which people have attached a thousand of the little "love locks"—throwing turtle shells out into the bay. They're drinking and joking, and the intermingled sound of clinking glass and strident, cawing laughter carries on the onshore wind. I guess the love platitudes are the butt of their jokes, messages on padlocks worn and rusted by the salty air, promises made by lovers standing before these marshes in former times. Though it could just as well be nerves, that they've heard of another dead peer and it's dawned on them they probably won't be far behind. Out beyond the rocky headland you can just make out the half-submerged ruins of the shipyard. Looming, soot-encrusted former warehouses and slips, and dykes whose flooded sluices now host massive flotillas of seaweed and Atlanti-Kola bottles that in turn host flocks of migrating birds. Beyond that, a whole lot of nothing. Solitary wooden planks float about where once, at the beginning of the last century, wood was worked with unparalleled mastery, until an explosion took place—a huge series of explosions—at the tripping of a naval minefield at a nearby base. All the old sea dogs claim it was for the best: business was on the slide, they say, following the influx of contractors from the east and their bargain-basement production costs. The sector was badly in need of diversification and, luckily, along came the Ż-Bug to finish that job. Neither are there any signs of life in the old huts that the sailors built while awaiting the reconstruction of the docks, at which time they weren't really sailors anymore, but mere tenders of storm lamps, hunkering in futile bunkers, though later on it was they who gave the Fishing Federation its heft, made it a force, versed as they were in the impossible-to-budge Atlantikan sedentaryism, the peculiar force-fulness of those who have run aground inside this slow unfolding of disease and tropics, tropics and disease. The huts, for all their lovely estuary views, appear void of lighting. Rows of identical barred windows, "For Rent" boards, and not a single sign of life, no shadows moving behind curtains or curtains twitching, no one stealing fur-tive looks at anything. The old Merchant Marine College overlooks this section of the docks (known locally as the Bazaar, since you used to be able to buy and sell just about anything there, especially if you were interested in doing so duty-free), its activities having long since transferred to Puerto Lombardo. Morgan's father, an ensign with bad eyes who never actually went to sea, used to teach mari-time law to second-year students at the college. When it declared bankruptcy and closed its doors, following a vigorous, devastating audit that uncovered a slew of tax-avoiding irregularities—to the tune of eleven million Credits—Morgan's father, rather than let it get to him or decide to walk the plank, or indeed just find a job at another maritime institution, took his redundancy as a sign: finally it was a chance for him to realize his dreams by weighing anchor and heading out across the seas. He bid farewell to his loved one, promising he'd return within the year, and adding that he planned to bring back chests full of precious stones and other goodies. He boarded a Malaysian freighter and was never seen in these waters again. He did, though, send Morgan regular postcard updates on his adventures—though they always took months to gain postal service clearance. The messages read like the captain's log of some legendary corsair, and the last one to make it through was sent from somewhere in deepest Cambodia, where it seemed he had set up as a trader in fabrics and textiles. Every time we broke up for vacation, Morgan announced that his father was about to send him a ticket, any day now, so he could go and visit the palace he was due to inherit, though our vacations always turned out exactly the same: an endless mire of boredom, sand, and sun. Days went by, the seasons turned, and the early hints of summer would once more remind Morgan of his presumptive Eastern expedition. Then a year came when he didn't mention it, and none of us could bring ourselves to either.

20.

We'd clear away our carpentry tools and drag ourselves back to our normal classroom, fingers bristling with splinters and sweaters covered in sawdust. Each and every particle trapped in the weave of the polyester seemed to cry out Indonesia, and something in each of us called back in unison: Jakarta. In my mind it was a deserted city made of glass, suspended in the clouds. Or a metropolis all of gold, nestled in a snow-covered valley. The palace of Ming the Merciless: Jakarta, Destroyer of Men. That was before. Now all I get in the images the stone gives me are extreme close-ups of the nun's wrinkles, the high ceilings and the damp spots in the corners, my schoolmates stuck clammily to their high-varnish desk seats. I think of those who felt the call and abandoned this city, of Fatty Muñoz, his shoulders like our pambazo bread—reddish and puffy—from so many beatings, of el Chino Okawa and his army of pet bedbugs, of Morgan and his grimaces, of Zermeño, Sparky, Birdface Helguera, whereabouts unknown: we assumed he had either been made prisoner to an olive-colored uniform and buzz cut, or was banging his head against the padded walls of a different kind of institution, eyes like that of a sated young calf. I think of all who quit the city when the quarantine came down. Of those scattered along the shore, stomachs distended and crawling with maggots, tongues sticking out at bizarre angles. But more than anything I think of those who remain, those who stayed on: forget about streets being named after them; the only thing they've gotten is older. Apart from the dockside esplanade, this city is split up into a million minor byways, each lasting no more than a couple of blocks before the roots of some palm tree tear up the sidewalk anyway, so really we could call them by whatever fucking name we want . . . It's just organization. Say we start low, one of our many flyblown squares, or some avenue no one really goes down. Even better: a central reservation. The problem being that even these are taken, former health secretaries and safe-seat members of parliament whose contribution in combatting the Ź-Bug took the form of writing out checks from their sterilized fortieth-story sanctums, complete with balconies, a long, long way up, is what I'm trying to say, and meanwhile where were we? In the shitty bowels. No, to get a street named after you around here you either need to have a half-decent Vakapý career behind you, or to have pushed pens in some office with great distinction. Of the exterminators, surprise, surprise: no sign. Not even an anonymous statue to commemorate all that went on, not one.

21.

Farther along the coast, beyond the ravines, the sky glows with a dirty light, like halogen lamps about to give up the ghost. There're the sailing clubs, then you come to Cabo Frío, then the beaches. That was where I first saw Clara, seemingly recently emerged from the Atlantik, wending her way between palm trees. Where Calle Ruiz-Cuevas meets Avenida Doctor Narváez, it breaks off in ten different directions. One of those thoroughfares, Calle 14 de Octubre, splits off into Matuk-Bayram, and that, as you approach the old mill, becomes Talabarteros, which in turn leads to the Old Town, former ceremonial center of the city and the place where conspirators hid away to do their conspiring, also once the location of the gallows and the place where the heads of criminals and infidels were mounted on stakes—entertainment for the non-criminals and non-infidels—as well as the Źocalo, the huge square bounded on each side by pointed archways evocative of colonial times, a spirit otherwise scoured away by centuries of storms and pillaging. Nowadays the Źocalo is occupied by the tents of hundreds if not thousands of protestors and lined with government offices, gaming centers, drinking joints and oyster bars alike, phone booths, the Cathedral of Our Lady of the Chrysalids, with its metal pilings that, according to the Institute of Capture, Processing, and Information Access, sink a little over twelve centimeters into the littoral alluvium each year, and, out in the middle of the square, the city's flag, the raising and lowering of which take place according to a strict schedule carried out by a group of consecrated conscripts, with all the power their military garb suggests—a group whose labors never reach an end, who raise and lower and neatly fold that flag seemingly nonstop, and who march about the square to the turning of the shadow of the flagpole. I think sometimes of the people who *should* be here—it's like they never were, like the sole historical inhabitants are those you see now, the protestors, the street vendors and their children, the endless line of the unemployed whose proficiencies are written in marker on pieces of cardboard, the displaced persons with their tents and signs. Perhaps you wouldn't be able to tell them apart anyway now; perhaps in this roiling mass of bodies they'd just blend in. They came down from Cordillera Hill because there was no place for them anywhere else. Some decided to stay on after the Ź-Bug passed and by now can't even remember what they're doing here. Naturally the Atlantika state of being, the inelegant civility that marks us out, starts to become their way of being also. It would take more than half an hour to walk the full circumference of the Żocalo, so I decide to pick my way directly through the tents instead. From among the canvas sheets hands reach up, trying to rob anything they can, a phone, a scrap of clothing. I quicken my step, though the terrain stays much the same. Perhaps it's the energy of this old center, its old and new and frenetic vibrations, that explains the fragmentariness of the adjacent streets, the way they endlessly fork and overlap and sometimes come to an abrupt dead-end only to pick up again a few blocks farther on, and in particular the constant and illogical name changes of what are essentially different portions *of the same street*. An occupational hazard for those of us in the Ź-Brigade, this unplanned city plan, the aleatory arterial interlocking of the city. We ended up learning to navigate by the sound of the wind and of the extractors, to always have a sense of where we were in relation to the coast and to simply retrace our steps according to that.

22.

Clara, she trembles. I can hardly take my eyes off her. When the fan bursts into life, she falls still, and vice versa, so that by the time a session ends there is a lag between them of nearly half a minute. Then the images suddenly stop—or, in fact, I think they stay precisely where they are, available to her if she wants to call on them, but the moment the link is broken between her and the pink light *I* cease to see them. After these months of watching, I can now predict exactly when it's about to happen. The static makes the hairs on her forearms stand up while simultaneously she begins to tremble, at moments so vigorously that her ponytail comes out and eventually the hair on her head hangs loose at her shoulders while a puddle of sweat begins to form around her feet on the lino. The undulating light from the stone ceases; the images freeze. Clara, between me and the stone, gets up and looks admiringly at the bones. And at the vase, and the coins. The dog. She lets me do her hair again. It's lost its former luster and is beginning to fall out in clumps. This is a job I relish: I begin rationalizing the mussed and tangled locks (though naturally the occasional strand does come away). I proceed as follows: first of all I split the whole head of hair in two with a clean line down the center. Take one thin section and cross it onto the other side, then bring a section from the other side back across, bring the first section over that, repeat. Don't pull too hard, but also leave out as few strands as possible. Repeat until you come to the faded tips, and finish it off with the tortoiseshell brooch. A handful of loose hair will end up scattered by your feet. All of it, today's hair and yesterday's and the hair from the day before, will eventually join together with the grime we bring in on our shoes, grains of sand, and the sleep we rub from our eyes, and make one of those little forgotten clumps of fuzz that go tumbling across the Llano, the great inland plain. The stone is bigger now. About the size of a six-year-old child. Clara does not know whether it fell from the sky or washed up from the Atlantik. Her idea is that it could have been an instrument, or one facet of a larger instrument, belonging to the true native inhabitants of this place, true children of the gods, or maybe even belonging to the Albýnos. And because its function wasn't immediately obvious, she at first interpreted it as part of some fractured symbol: one fragment of a larger, no longer fully available code. I thought she had to be crazy, for all that she was able to demonstrate, through various tests, that it drowned out all sound and the wind itself. That discovery did shake me, above all because though you can live with the noise of this city—or rather, though you have to live with it, by it, have eventually to become it—and though nobody around here actually very much wants to be alive anymore, for once that ambient din came to a halt, and for the first time in as long as either of us could remember we were able to clear our heads. This room has been a space of silence ever since. The stone fulfills two functions, as proof of the overall deterioration, the damage and decline, but also as holder for all our energies—not so much our hopes; we long since gave those up. This was why, or how, Clara tuned in to the stone—about two months ago now. Then we knew it wasn't just for protection; it was also a message: it had chosen us—or whoever sent it had, whether native inhabitants or Albýnos—and not the other way around.

23.

Then the nun would say: Guyana. And someone would always fall for it and think she meant French Guiana. And the rest of us, idiots that we were, would respond with a sharp intake of breath. Oh, those wrinkles. She'd talk and we'd have no option but to listen, trying to make sense of the sounds that filtered out through the cracks in her face. The soul, she said, is composed of a material that will never degrade: it is housed inside the body but in no way does it belong to the body. Nor does the soul expire in concert with the body, except in the case of suicide. With suicide, the soul stays trapped within this slab of flesh, this greasy wad of meat—and what, children, what is meat without any soul? I'll tell you: hamburgers. Nothing but hamburgers. And thereafter the meat rots and the soul leaves it behind, but slowly, oh so slowly, falling dim over the eons, like all the many unmoving things.

24.

Groups of the Magnetiźed stream past with heads lowered, minds on their supplications, what it is they will ask for today. They are on their way to the old Anguja court. I don't know in detail what rites they observe or the articles of their faith. To me they all seem alike; I feel like they all hail from the same faraway location, some place human in scale and utterly governed by superstition. Their Ministerź cast mistrustful looks at my bare wrists, this being their attitude to any who fail to display their symbols. To them all Vakapýists are offensive in the eyes of god (their god). All who lay bets, all who drink, all who absent themselves from the consecrated fields in and around the Anguja without permission: any who have refused the blessings of magnetiźation. Which makes it strange, to say the least, that they should have chosen the hull of the old Anguja as their gathering place. One article of their faith I do know about, though it's said that rather than converts they seek allies, is that Albýnos are not allowed to join. A cult with neither novices nor a catechism for them to learn. A hint of this new faith's mercantile roots can be discerned in its practices, which posit the congregation as the clientele. They function more like affiliates than as members of a religion: stakeholders in their own benightedness. While the adults congregate before the homily loudspeakers formerly used by the Mirasol Corporation to promote its wares, the young cluster together like leeches at the approach of any outsider. Their faces are snot encrusted, their ill-shaped clothes hang off their shriveled bodies. They try to foist bracelets on me of all colors and sizes, they want me to buy their prayer books, their little knapped magnetic stones, knives, daggers, necklaces, ring pulls. The Anguja rears up behind them, victim of its former glories. I have never seen it except for in its current state, the walls inches thick in bird shit, top to bottom. By the time I was old enough to start going along to matches, the Department of Chaos and Gaming had set in motion the new Vakapý plan and the very first gaming stations were sending gamblers into ecstasies. The place fell into disuse until the Magnetiźed decided to start congregating there. As boys we used to see the results in Helguera's newspapers, and the images of the playérs, striding about the courts or with wreaths and massive champagne bottles after a win, gave us the idea of the Anguja as the embassy of some other world, irrefutable proof that a different reality was possible, far removed from the one we inhabited with its constant school fundraisers and constant empty stomachs. In those days we still believed we deserved to be lucky, and that one day we surely would be. The Anguja, while completely out of reach, nonetheless seemed to offer a kind of exemption from normal Atlantika life; we'd never get there ourselves, but it was still of this earth, still somehow at hand. Whereas Grandma used to go regularly during the Anguja's golden era. When her first husband died she developed a liking for the game and became a devoted follower, hardly ever missing a Sunday match; the dead man had seen it as a vice, not befitting churchgoing Chrysalids, partly in fact because he hailed originally from the Sierra, where Vakapý inspires nothing like the mania it does here. Look now, Grandma, it's your pupa here: see what's become of the paragon of our Atlantikan ways, this crumbling and forgotten edifice, lit by the putrid glow of a city that itself endures only thanks to the wholesale submission of its inhabitants to the founding principles: seclusion, indifference, and a stubborn get-powerful-quick mentality.

25.

It happened two months ago. I came back after two nights straight at the gaming station. It's like that when you're on a roll, and even— sometimes especially—when you aren't. In closed matches there can be over a thousand bets laid, and that's before you take into account those from other divisions. The key is to pick matches with the maximum amount of data to study, and then, of course, it's down to your ability to judge and interpret the possible fallout of each play. Not everyone's got it. The smallest movement, down to the flick of a player's wrist, can generate a further series of digits that affect the bets, and can in turn themselves be betted on. The modern game no longer has human bookmakers; computers have stepped in to calculate the odds—a computer, in fact, originally developed by the War Institute to analyze ballistics trajectories but that has wound up as the sole administrator of the impulses and bad luck of your average Atlantikan betting addict. You need very little in order to gather and send out the data that will then be aggregated and classified via the hundreds of thousands of cables and wires running from the official franchises, all the tens of thousands of stationery stores, taverns, and kiosks. So it must be, according to Vakapý competition laws: any establishment with a properly calibrated gaming station and a banking terminal has the right to register bettors and become an official partner in the Department of Chaos and Gaming syndicate. Vakapý is an easy game to learn, hence the appeal, hence the huge number of addicts. At certain intervals two numbers are assigned: 10 for the favorites, who then play in blue, and 9 for the challengers, who get put in red. In the rare cases when each side comes into a match on an identical winning or losing run, and on equal points in the league, the kits are assigned according to whichever team's name comes first in the alphabet. The odds are announced a few minutes before the start whistle and constantly update on the basis of bets placed and the ever-changing in-game stats: shots, service, sacks, activity zones, ground pickups, number of errors per game, shots from players' stronger or weaker hands, average velocities, carambolas, use of the walls: minute by minute, every variant reduced to chains of numbers whose sole function is to prolong the deep pleasure people take in throwing away their money, whether they be first-timers struggling to keep up with the plays or inveterate high rollers laying everything on the line, one last time, again. There are nearly 750 different kinds of plays you can bet on but no limit to the number of calls you can make at any given point, which makes it a rare thing indeed for any person to sit down to a game—even someone who "doesn't really care for it," or the supposed "take it or leave it" types—and not stay put for days or even weeks, and furthermore usually have not a single Credit to their name by the end. I came back to the room late in the day after a particularly punishing stint and found Clara taking a rest on the mattress, under a thin sheet through which her prone, sweating form could be seen. At that time Clara could still find rest after her sessions with the stone. Her bones still had some flesh on them, and she sheened with the recent discovery of the stone's capacity to keep out noise, a scintillance that ran over her shoulders and down to the tips of her fingers, less restive and claw-like than they later became. She spent long hours trying to decipher her incipient enthrallment to the stone, to understand its properties and the way it behaved, and would later subside onto the mattress with a low groan. The springs of the mattress would barely register her arrival. The evening in question unfortunately found me in a good mood. Señora Albýno#2460 had treated me well—no sexual favors, there hadn't even been any touching of hair, but she'd looked after me all the same, lifting the heavy cloud that had installed itself after a succession of woeful bets. When I came in Clara got up and returned to her task. I apologized for having been gone so long but she barely seemed to hear. My mind had been full of

Señora Albýno#2460—how sad her pink eyes made me, how bleak her absence of melanin always seemed to me—but in an instant the stone honed in on me and emptied my mind of all thoughts. I quietly crossed the room and crouched down beside Clara. Within a couple of seconds I couldn't move. And a short while later—I couldn't say how long precisely—I began to see them: they were tiny and made their way across an area whose edges were faint and stippled, like the tracings on a map. No taller than my pinkie finger, just like el Chino Okawa's pet bedbugs. A building appeared, half transparent as well. I rubbed my eyes, could I be dreaming: the plan of a building, some place containing a massive trash heap, possibly, or a Vakapý court or a factory, or all three at once, superimposed; the framework, pillars, and concrete pilings with netting around them, the skeleton of the original building indistinguishable from the one, or ones, that would eventually replace it. The contours overlapped without blocking each other out, and above them stood another phantasmagorical edifice, directly atop the blackened, red-brick walls (red as the driven snow). And to one side, infinitesimal, the boys—walking around, all puppy fat and prepubescence. While the vision lasted I was able to zoom in and out on any detail I chose by dint of some oiled cogs presented to me on a kind of crane spar. But I still found it impossible to date the footage and its conjectural perspectives. The summer before the novice? A couple before, or even the one after? Our faces were intermittently visible, and as the vision grew darker in color and the contrast increased I was gradually able to tell the boys apart—at first they were little more than blurry, shifting shadows, all much alike, little more than hasty lines strewn across overexposed graph paper, a cluster of whites, or even some kind of white boat docked in between the zinc tiles, the contours of the building, or its foundations. But it was them. So small, so fragile. I watched for a long time as they wandered around looking lost. Then, in single file, they turned and went inside the factory. Clara studied me, or she looked through my flesh, supervising or inspecting the levels, brightness and contrast. And everything bathed in pinkest light.

26.

Today the Anguja counts as one more ghostly presence in our architecture of abeyance. Its sturdy, rectilinear facade is divided up by columns, at the center of which is a loose semicircle of transparent vitroblocks bearing the building's name, written in fluoride— still discernible in spite of the layers of graffiti, the ingrained soot and mud, and the great forest of bindweed that has grown up after so many decades of neglect. The west stand, once decorated with enormous protruding concrete disks, steel, and double-paned glass, has been demolished. There was a time when the circular structure functioned as a rotating cocktail bar, split into three parts, each of which turned in opposite directions; nowadays all that remains of the machine at the center of the gaping hole is its exposed terminal and a rotor blade from a family car, corroded and completely stripped of functional parts, semiconcealed behind a trio of wire fences erected by the police in a long-ago effort to stop people from coming in. Some of the greatest, most brutal Vakapý matches ever took place in the Anguja, but now its crumbling walls give sanctuary to the Magnetiźed. I don't know when they first arrived, but it would have been a similar story to all the other places they have colonized over time. The government does nothing, adjudging them a minor threat at most: they're on the electoral roll, they don't cause trouble, they keep themselves to themselves. It has been the same in all the many cinemas and theaters, which, having stood empty, become the homes for multifarious factions unresistant to occasionally being gathered up by government forces and bused to polling booths. Faith, after all, is a natural filler for multiuse venues. The only one with a greater capacity than the Anguja is the old mill. The geometric designs, with the xolo-monsters and Anubis-like dogs eating their own tails, seem directly inspired by Mayan and Egyptian iconography, though now these have been torn down and replaced by welded brass effigies depicting the miracles of magnetiźation. Only one or two people still alive in the neighborhood around the Anguja can recall its heyday. It's one of dozens of ruins whose hulking forms, half-destroyed or half-built, stud the shoreline, and a place where people apparently used to flock on a daily basis, from the great and the good to those who aspired to greatness or goodness, and everyone in between: in the VIP boxes, they called out their bets with the same vulgar ferocity as everyone else in the stadium, the only difference, except for their smart outfits and the hideous plastic surgery of the wives and girlfriends, being that they were intent on losing not only their own money but also that of the people they were supposed to represent in the corridors of power—the clerks, delegates and subdelegates, boxers with cosmetic reconstructions, impresarios, builders, stars of screen and big top spread out below them, and those below them also, the anonymous tourist class, a dark sea of heads, hunters of favorable odds all—*taxpayers all*—writhing like fish in the whorls of steam rising from the sweating, polyester-clad bodies. Such were the scenes in the Anguja. And because cement, whatever pretty designs one may wish to embellish it with, will never lose its binding, synthetic properties—will never stop being cement—the Anguja has been able to serve as both sports field and temple, and could just as well be a prison or an anonymous, multipurpose events space. It has never been fully demolished for the same reason no one is ever going to properly restore it. In this city nothing ever materializes in full, just as nothing ever truly goes away. What would be the point of rebuilding something destined only to remain half-finished, whose completion dates are bound to enter the twilight of endless deferment? No one was ever willing to take on the lease, thus the cement structure fit itself to the combined flows of time passing and generalized indifference. So it goes, and to oppose it would require a kind of responsibility-taking simply not part of our makeup. It sounds harsh, but isn't really: the moment cement dries, we in turn fit ourselves to whatever shapes it's been made into. Hence why in Atlantika we always choose to live among ruins rather than face the immeasurable trepidation of open spaces.

27.

The heat makes us see things. Things that aren't there, and never were. Like: the pinkie finger of a small boy whose body I found in a pile of trash, when we were out gathering the infected corpses one day. A fraction. The tiniest portion. A pinkie finger, among all that death— emphatic, categorical, large-scale death. What gives it such weight?

28.

This city has two great enemies: its inhabitants and the viruses they transport. Though the constant wind drives people out of their minds, and also carries viruses around, in no way can it be said to represent an evil in itself, for all its unpredictably and indeed the unpredictable effect it has on different people's temperaments. It springs up in some faraway location and brings sudden atmospheric changes, a pano-ply of electric charges, abrasions, and erosions. People say that the viruses would have no reason to exist if it weren't for humans, that they originate in our bodies and survive thanks to processes of intra-dermal decomposition, or through other cellular mechanisms they latch onto and finally begin to drive. Or if it weren't for the brain: that they arise in the brain of the person who fails to understand the parasitical paradise that is the body. The slightest chink and it begins—a sneeze, an itch, a damp patch; anything can be like a red carpet for devastating infecting agents like the Ź. And this city has always been a gateway to the continent for such bugs. The Albýnos were the worst offenders. The chroniclers from the times they first hove into view—as slaves on the invaders' boats—speak of a virus that decimated the populace; the natives, whose dark bodies would be painted shades of copper and violet, were alarmed at these vivid white arrivals and made it clear they were not in need of new neigh-bors, thank you very much. The virus, AKA the Á-Bug, AKA the invad-ers' greatest weapon; their smartest move was to simply wait for it to spread behind the enemy stockades. Really the damage was done the moment their pigmentless captives set foot on our beaches: vitamin-deficient and glowering, carrying their own shackles and reeking of rat piss, awash with cankers and ulcers. Even the little subcutaneous nicks, even these were enough once they had made their pact with the tropical heat and its consommé of diphtherias, brackish water, and humidity—oh, treacherous humidity. These little microarmies, too, jumped down from the ships and waded through the warm shallows, abandoning the snowy expanses of their hosts and seeking refuge in the virgin expanses of us. Then all the invaders had to do was wait. We could look at how closely packed together the native dwellings were, though the custom of maintaining a strict bathing regimen, whether in good health or otherwise, was certainly also bad news: much as the mestizos nowadays love to trumpet the virtues of regular ablutions, these supposedly hygienic practices were in fact the perfect opportunity for the Bug to spread. We read about it in *The Short Account of the Catastrophe at San Jacinto Itzcuintlán* by Don Bernardo Giménez de Ademuz, one of Fish Hook's absolute favorites and the man whose face adorns our fifty CRÐ bill: "Very many lost their lives and those who did avoid the full mortal Fury of the Illnesse were left as cripples and placed inside colonies alone, removed from human Contact for Tens of Years." It was the Á-Bug that laid the natives low, but the conquistadors went home as heroes all the same. Those who stayed on, the idiots who fell for some local beauty, or for the climate, or, worse, were transfixed by an old-world idea of prosperity, may have eventually become wealthy in these latitudes but mostly ended up losing it all anyway. So it went, a story or history (as you prefer) that began in the same way any entity covered in pustules is a beginning, and in a place where dead and rotting bodies soon stretched as far as the eye could see. Like this story. Like all stories. Johnny or Juan "Progress" knows what I mean: Ź-brigaðiers gathering bodies among the rocks. Men with plumed helmets having their wicked way with them. An all-too-heady mixture of fear, shamanism, and a lively trade in trinkets and precious metals.

29.

Clara takes me by the hand. I feel like we've been here before, many times. Like I talk about it, and then it happens again: like it happens while simultaneously I am talking about it. Her hands are bundles of stripped wire, the protruding veins a clear representation of what little energy remains in the battered resistor of her. It's today, then. Look, she says, her voice wavering: Pay attention. The vase is made of china, not thousands of years old but rather mass manu-factured at some point, and later exchanged for a rice bowl; the dog is a dog with short legs, small, low to the ground, so insignificant as to barely be worth thinking about. And that, I think, makes it more dangerous: a beggar for affection. Its belly almost drags on the ground, like the very lowest of creatures. The coins on the table and those inside the pocket could be omitted but something makes them shine, like brilliant points of light on the wooden tabletop. Then Clara's gums, red on black; her small white teeth; and after that her trembling hands. And I look. I look carefully. They seem welded together, the lines: no more stippling now, now we're seeing a far clearer picture. A burst of blinding light comes from the stone, directly onto Clara's forehead. It seems to make her skin duller than before, to add depth to the lines of her crow's feet and fur-rowed brow, all the blemishes and marks that fossilize old looks and expressions. Vulture light. The disappearance of the world, accord-ing to the stone, or according to our interpretation of its message, will be unremarkable in every way, a mere matter of processes— slow, rather orderly processes, one part of which is us agonizingly waiting our turn. I see myself leave the house, but the house as part of a spatial realm only, not temporal: so clear, so seemingly con-crete. It is no easy thing to see yourself and in the same instant to be asking: Is it really me walking along like that, all knock-kneed, like I've spent too long riding horses? It seems so genuinely ridicu-lous that I don't even feel I can take issue with the way I've been ren-dered, the thin head of hair on the projected me as he goes down the street—as *I* go down the street—in the direction of the docks, on my way to see if it's possible to find the final hiding place of my former comrades.

30.

From Morgan's notebook:

"On Lachtman's observations:

In the British Kaffraria the dead were left in the open air to be devoured by wolves, birds of prey, and insects. (Barrow, London, 1797)

In Hyrcania, street dogs would pick the flesh from the bones of the dead.

The Bactrians thought it acceptable to feed the infirm and the aged to the dogs. Hence mounds of bones rather than tombs have been uncovered in Bahl.

Zoroastrianism holds that bodies become contaminated when they die. When the body rots, that is an entry point for demons wishing to access the world of the living. To ward off such invasions they practiced *excarnation:* they built circular, raised structures known as Towers of Silence and placed dead bodies at the highest points, to be exposed to carrion birds. Once the birds, along with the elements, had scoured the bones, the bones would be taken out into the desert.

The Callatiae consumed the bodies of their dead parents. The Persian King Darius I asked a Greek attendant at his court for what price his people would eat their fathers' dead bodies. He answered that there was no price for which they would commit such a vile act. Darius then summoned the Callatiae and asked how much they would need to agree to burn their forebears' bodies on a pyre. The Callatiae cried aloud, saying such a thing would be sacrilege."

31.

I am going to meet up with the boys. I am going to try and find them. The stone tells me I must. First thing is to establish the exact stops, one by one, avoid any possibility of going wrong: really *know* the stops. I've memorized the numbers. But I'm not going from here—not in the slightest. In the vision-images, it seems like I am, but that's only the turbulence of Clara's mind. For all that the stone may seem like a lens or a portal, it is only a stone—hence the impossibility of resisting its commands. Everything before this journey that I'm now undertaking on foot is, or seems to be, part of an alien existence. Or at any rate like a beginning, but somehow tacked on, incompatible with this current moment—a period of time with the obvious whiff of fabrication, more a premonition than my actual history. This is the effect the stone has, breaking everything down and realigning it. The images solidify with surprising clarity, and not on the wall anymore but in midair: together they comprise the merest breach, a miniscule aperture, the tiniest rupture in the prehistoric physiognomy of the mineral. And what will happen, I ask. But nobody answers. Clara takes a deep breath, and she and the stone join in a long, slow exhalation. Her hands tremble, or seem to tremble. The heat makes us see things that aren't there.

32.

There are few surviving manuscripts that describe the native inhabitants and the adversities they faced. And these live in the vaults of the National Library. The west wing of the Palace of Congress bears a mural—fruit of a memorial project organized many years ago by the Department for Education and the National Office for Artistic Creations. The idea was to commemorate the painful chapters in our history, events that, according to an undersecretary in the Tourism Department, "saw us sift out, like gold prospectors, all the weakness inherent in these peoples." Unsurprisingly the project was plagued by friction among the union members who toiled (on double pay) to complete the noble work—they did not in fact complete it. While the bureaucrats and filing clerks accused the artists both of laziness and of trying to alter the historical accounts, the artists claimed censorship. The result: half-finished murals, later reworked as collages, daubed with religious messages and graffitied cocks: "Hardly was it possible to sow grain, given the great dearth even of seeds after so many bad harvests . . . And the tribes that paid us tribute were found to be so stubborn and so fond of their unruly ways, so attached even to the endless hunger and hardships that afflicted them, that our karaý-guazú was obliged to delve into the grain stores for foodstuffs put aside in former years, yet when the stores were examined they were found empty, for the terrible weevil worm had got there first . . . Yay foreign barbarians came from the North and razed all in their path, and fire fell from the sky and men's bodies were full of cankers . . . As our persecution continued and as winter came on we, too, set out on a journey to colder lands . . . The young men were charged with transporting the stone and did work tirelessly in this for the pursuers were swift and traveled without effects . . . By and by the elderly were left behind, and the sick and womenfolk also, as all of these were like a heavy weight around the necks of the stone-bearers . . . And our hearts pounded, like the rubber from the trees, and the dwelling places were left bare of people and in the land we came to the plants gave off rank malodorousness and the fruits were not good to eat, but there was nothing else, so eat them we did, and our distress was great, we had no furs to protect us from the cold, we had nothing that we needed . . . Our spears served only to scratch us on the backs . . . And then the stone gave out its augur: saying unto us that the flesh of men would be eaten, and that there would be no blame in this."

33.

From Morgan's notebook:

"And once a place was found the first misfortune came down upon us, the first of many . . . for the land was barren and the seeds sown there yielded naught but misery, and this in spite of the temples we built wherever the stone commanded, and many went away to consult with demons, but the demons gave more grievous answers still, for the men had shown little patience and less faith. Then the heavens sent down torments and there were droughts also . . . The karaý-guazú decided to alter the year, for the year of the rabbit had been one of woe, and so a new year was added to the calendar . . . The time for planting seeds came and there was a plague of locusts and the people went hungry . . . They were driven to consort with the settlers, who had created dwelling places for themselves, and even sold their children into bondage or promised to sell the children they were yet to bear . . . and the next year there was a plague of rats and the next a plague of gophers, and the next year there was great sickness, and the next year there was flooding throughout the lands . . . Those men still remaining went into neighboring regions to find provisions and into the forests, too, but very often they did not return and their lives were consumed by great weariness and by hunger and misery."

34.

People want to know about the rats. About the days and nights we spent underground. I say to them: the sounds emitted by rats are part of a complex system of signals that the human ear cannot properly decipher. One of the leaders of the Ź-Brigađe, Kovac the Albýno, said that a long and detailed study would allow you to analyze the creatures' language, and that even if such a study weren't possible, and although many of the sounds they made were inaudible to us, you could still discern direct links between the alpha's squeaked commands and the activity of the group. Avalanche! Kovac would suddenly cry, his ear to the bunker wall, trying to make out those rodent signals, warped somewhat but amplified, too, by the drainage pipes. Then the walls would rumble and shake, and the rest of us would hit the deck, always too late. Listen, Kovac would hiss. You can understand them, you just need to become part of them, you just need to *feel* them. But none of the rest of us could, partly because none of the rest of us were Albýno: employed for so many generations as miners, their sensitivity to auditory stimuli has been altered by hundreds of years' proximity to the earth's magnetic fields. This meant it was incredibly useful to have Kovac in the unit, though any time we went above ground the sun also made him something of an impediment. He had played Vakapý in his younger days: he was one of the first Albýno ever granted a license to play at the Anguĵa. He had a couple of good seasons before an elbow injury forced him into early retirement. He kept a trading card inside his locker: a streak of white leaning against the front wall of a court, ahaka in his right hand and a smile bringing the color down a few notches. His was a generation in sepia, skin versus stone: epic stories of the greats putting down the ahaka and challenging each other to glove throws and, once the sponsors had paraded past, the balls had been selected, and the court sanctified, sweating out the previous night's wine, and the wine from all the nights before: 190 BPM on a court measuring just 62 meters in length. Bullshit, I say if anyone asks me. Give me the stats, I say. On a rest day once, Kovac told us that after his retirement, having by then spent many years drinking himself into what looked likely to be an early grave, someone from a TV channel came to see him and offered him a part in *Strains,* a miniseries to be produced by the State Channel, aimed at raising awareness about the

Albýno. And he did end up taking part: who better to demonstrate the sporting successes of his race and thereby validate their rise to social acceptability? And the series, more a sitcom than anything, was popular. For instance, there was an Albýno woman who used to wash my family's feet, and after the first few episodes, Grandma, having spent several afternoons in tears at the iniquities of our ancestors, started addressing her by her first name. Public spirited, and networked at prime time. Kovac, dear Kovac: the pain is real if the ratings say it is. And you, who said so little about yourself, and far too much about the rats and the musical-gnawing notations. Kovac was the only one who, when the Ź-Bug entered its final stages, saw (heard) that it was in fact still active: only he had learned to appreciate the nuances in the silence that the rest of us had little time for, or feared, or failed to notice altogether, a silence without any drumroll that he himself would have disregarded had he not been immersed in it, up to his neck in the muddy slime of it. I don't know how he ended up in the Brigades, but I suspect solitude had something to do with it. Solitude, the education system, the Credit system, the judicial system. And yet, no, there's no blame to assign, only systems. It has become the fashion to renounce life as merely one more system, though all that really achieves is to put life and system in the same breath. I find these terms the most useful when thinking about Kovac as well: implacable will to survive, unsullied by mutations or the betting life, suffering both from the purity of his race and the attendant ocular difficulties, capable of going out on exercises over and over, again and again, filling up the sacks, emptying out the sacks. The same goes for each of the bodies decomposing along the coast, every pinkie finger and arm and bodiless head we collected, every rat's tail: I consider it all part of a force that had no purpose other than to impose itself, trampling the supposed obstacles of bodies, of bones, of spirits, broken all of them, broken and drained of blood and nameless, and because nameless therefore belonging to us all, or to those who came before us and who are also now part of us. A systematic solitude. It was Kovac who surmised that, once the

Ź-Bug was rampant, it prompted the colony to begin operating like an automaton. Not the scientists, not the government, not the petulant bureaucrats or scholars, but one of us: this rum-soaked, more than half-blind Vakapý veteran, in debt to everyone, expected to pay for all manner of things, even his five minutes of fame when a public TV channel used him in their cack-handed attempt to suborn the nation's past. Kovac said: We'll stop hearing them now, they'll be at a lower ebb and will stop moving around so much, they won't even be hungry now because only the living experience hunger . . . Morgan had his own take on the importance of distinguishing the long screeches from the short, considering it a given that the sickness normalized the noises, made them all sound the same. A deeper pitch, a sharper tone: all were part of one single thing, one conglomerated mass, of which we were also part. But once the Ź-Bug had begun to affect their motor skills and their brain functions had all but shut down—those shitty little brains, impelled by untold electrical impulses—the rats, too, fell silent. At times all we'd hear of them would be the clicking together of teeth somewhere in the depths, luring their own prey. That sounded different, someone would say, and a shiver would run through us—shiver after shiver. We longed for the way things had once been: more violent, but at least not so unbearably quiet. In the beginning. Which beginning? At least the rats were a way of measuring the passage of time.

35.

As the National Archives show, for all that the "progressives" tried to argue otherwise, the country was on the slide. Largely this was down to the fact that the bodies we inhabit have a unique capacity for generating new and ever more complex fermentation methods—something the priests never bothered to tell us much about. The native inhabitants had some strange ideas on this count. Their view was that any deviation from the natural order was the work of noncorporeal agents who acted according to divine will. These were seen as operating within a pyramidal hierarchy not dissimilar to the one governing our society, with the lowest caste, those with physical disabilities and skin conditions, required to purge their own bodies by self-flagellation. The Bug, in its earliest instances, arrived from another continent, but it was here that it found its optimum environment. We should be honest about this. Mestizo thinking commonly blames our plight on barbarians, savages, outsiders. Our city may nowadays overflow with corporate offices, police stations, and Vakapý stadia, and that may well be unhealthy, but it suffered afflictions long before the first settlers showed up: we know that every winter the indigenes went up to the cordillera to try to shake off whichever treponema was troubling them at the time. We call it Cordillera Hill now, it's got its own zip code as well as semidrinkable water and a "sanitation" system, but it was once known simply as the cordillera: a few blackish mounds of earth slightly higher than sea level, scattered with unprepossessing boulders. Formerly a site of sacrifices, former rites: attempts, in other words, to keep longstanding barren spells at bay, to avert sicknesses and other endemic catastrophes.

36.

Beasts of burden were routinely sacrificed, but if the countryside refused to yield crops or if there had been a plague, they would have little objection to dispatching the occasional first-born child or virgin, whichever there happened to be more of. It needs to be understood that among the great nations (and we Atlantikans have always labored under the illusion of greatness—no less weighty for being a total fiction) virginity has never been held in particularly high esteem, and there are always more than enough children to go round. Burnt offerings in the shape of minors could even be seen as a noble gesture, given the high esteem in which the very young, along with the fat, were held. (Any individual born with what we would consider mental disabilities, or with a wizened face, would also be revered.) The ritual, carried out with the utmost gravity and extremely demanding for all involved, unfolded over the course of several days. *Report on the Southern Lands,* "a most faithful account of the discovery, conquest, and conversion of the Indians," written by Doctor Don Antonio Funes y Almanza, Count of Traslomita and Senior Judge and Census Keeper on behalf of the Royal Court of New Seville (the guy on the ten CRĐ note), describes it in the following way: "And here is the Truth of how these Men were able to live more than one life: they painted their bodies using indelible inks and spent great effort in the Decoction of certain plants that the karaý-guazú or headman spent many days brewing and preparing, and the imbibing of it was aimed at no other thing than to acquire Powers of Divination, to hear the Song of the Spheres and divers other Deceptions . . . And the Herbs being ground together and heated over fires, the Elders and those couples joined in most unholy matrimony came and took their places and sought to drive hence their vexations by the burning of bushels of the Copal tree and of Ephedra . . . Next came forth the Men whose office it was to tup the maidens and this Atrocity they carried out, maddened in the great billowings of heady smoke and Ignorant of civil ways and the existence of the Lord and Ignorant of the paths of reason they henceforth drank the Decoctions and in this wise did abandon the World . . . When the Imagination is as it were decollated from the Body it may commit most irresponsible Acts and range into Deliriums and it is well known by all who fear God that no form of good fortune nor yet of Grace may bring them out of the darkness then, for their Bodies, as it were void of thought, began to mount one another in great writhing piles, and their Humors were all mixt ere the vile carving and chopping up of their bodies commenced." Quite the feast: palm hearts, yucca, corn, sugarcane, bananas, tejocote seeds, the flowers of the spiky biznaga, leg of tapir, and, as the main course, a child whose body had been torn up and scattered around. The limbs, flesh, and viscera would adorn the ritual space and the slope leading up to it, and the celebrants would pick them up and dance around with them, swinging the bloody remains in time to the frenzied rhythm of drummers brought in from the area nowadays known La Collera. The general idea being that it was better to be ingested by one of your kin than become an incubator for maggots. The Albýno were yet to make an appearance at this point. They doubtless would have been added to the sacrificial mix, but before the migrations, we were strictly people of the sun. A shame. Albýno children and fat kids: surely an offering any god would be hard pressed to ignore.

37.

We waited for them to group together. We were a tiny crew at first. Kovac, Morgan, one or two besides. People think it was an easy job. Evacuating buildings. Going around in Day-Glo outfits. Maybe that was why they treated us like plumbers. We collected their dead children. We cleaned their dead children. We numbered, arranged, and made a final resting place for their dead children. Plumbers, they called us, dogsbodies, handymen. True, if a place is infested, you fumigate using sodium cyanide and sulfuric acid. OK, so why the fuss? Our instructions were simple, but carrying them out was far from it: first evacuate, then wait two days to see if the chemicals have an effect—any harmful excess will dissipate in that time—and the tenants or workers may then return to their homes or places of work. The training Morgan and I received was old school in the extreme. Patience isn't for everyone, but nothing beats it for effectiveness. You don't need much of a brain to carry out a massacre, but that isn't extermination: extermination takes skill. Apart from anything, the dead pests have to disappear completely, quickly followed by you. Your average José doesn't much like to ponder death—hence the Ź-Brigades. It was possible to think of ourselves as a community service, a group charged with keeping the mental peace, with keeping the Noble Empire (the economy) humming along. Of course: massacres are no good for business.

38.

From Morgan's notebook:

"And the Syphilitic and the Lepers scaled the mountain on all fours and once their most weary limbs had reached the Summit, they diligently cleaned the Altars or did whatever task was given to them. These unfortunate souls, truly little more than Skin and Bones, did wash themselves with great carefulnesse and were not minded to change their Condition (a state they had long ago accepted as deserving and Innate) but rather sought to prevent the worsening of it. It was, then, the habit among them to keep their skin of utmost cleanliness, above all because this same Idol to which they commended their cankers and sores was believed to be the One to smite them bodily should they fail to venerate this Devil."

39.

In a way our work was pure potluck. We were dependent on so many things, from the toxicology tests to the weather, to ambient noise, to the strictly demarcated zones within which we were authorized to carry out our searches, and to agonizing assessments and analyses based on sheer coincidence—on strings of numbers that, though random, would soon repeat or seem to match up with something or other and immediately be given the label "data": you could, if you stared hard enough, discern hazy correlations or similitudes of some kind, and, real or not, at least they gave us something to go on. Because when we were down below, blind luck and its manifestations trumped logic every time, and we flipped a hell of a lot of coins. All of which meant, down on our bellies in the murk and shit, we did everything we could to refine our intuitional capacities, particularly if it was a day when luck didn't seem to be on our side, and that was most days. At first we worked along the same lines as conventional fumigators, dipped pieces of bread in milk and rat poison—hours we spent doing that, making that milky-arsenic mush. It's a minor outbreak, you morons, they said. Evidence negligible. Patterns of activity? Dream on. So get to it: dip that bread. Dip it, and go gather dead bodies, they said. That was always the line. Nothing to worry about. We've seen worse. Remember '58? And we did remember, impossible not to, for all that many of us weren't even born then. Our bug, the Ź, proved resistant to most of the poisons we tried, but obviously we had to try them first. An antidote was cooked up, and the bacteria shuddered in response. We trusted in the approach until it became clear, all too clear, that the situation was more complicated than our betters had realized. In normal cases, your average infestation, the poison takes awhile, but the job's a clean one. Barium carbonate: ninety centigrams does it, though patience is still a must. They can smell it, so you have to starve the fuckers first: starvation is the only way to truly take them out. The young are easier to trick—accustomed to the mother's teat, they haven't learned to be as wary, and they'll eat whatever they come across. The mother is a harder nut to crack. If she does take the bait, the poison goes to work only gradually, and while she's on her way out, the little ones are likely to go snuffling around for food—bingo. It isn't rocket science, but you do need to learn how to wait. Sometimes, when the pink light becomes too much for my eyes and I am forced to momentarily look away from the vision, or when Clara breaks off for whatever reason, to cough, or because a fly crosses the room, landing on some spandex item of clothing, or on a bra, or on whatever forms have manifested in the room over the course of afternoon and evening, leading to a break in the transmission, the thought comes: that it was they who were being patient with us and not the other way around. Good old rats. Or patient old rats,

at least, which if you take everything else into account should probably be a sufficient substitute for actual goodness. Go on boys, the rats
were saying, you'll be heroes, they'll name streets after you, and we'll
still have the run of our kingdom underground. Patience, though,
whether exhibited by humans or other species, always runs out in
the end. It is finite. At some point, and nobody can say when it'll
be, all the sanguine logic in the world must also give up. Kovac was
right. There was a point at which they stopped acting according to
the simple causal chains to which it is possible to reduce all plagues.
There weren't any more mother rats, there weren't any more of their
offspring, there were no litters, nests, or colonies at large beneath the
streets of Atlantika; a point came when they were nothing but small,
unaffiliated furies, flying where they would.

40.

The blades have stopped turning. It's hot, and they've stopped, the
fan has given up, possibly it's falling to pieces, but certainly it isn't
working. Even though it's hot. Terribly hot, terribly stopped. The
dust has become encrusted on the blades, liable soon to be so thick
it reaches the wall. The stone is currently showing an old advertise-
ment for Mirasol bracelets, with a slogan so cloying that it survived
for generations and eventually, thanks to the power of nostalgia,
attained cult status: a couple in their thirties, very sexy, in sporty
clothes, in a big house, big garden out back, hammock out front,
clean car out front, clean dog, clean kids, pastel shades, everything
bright and shining. *The bracelets that make us happy, the bracelets
that fill us with pulsing life. Mirasol bracelets.* A great gushing surge
of good fortune and happiness, manumission and serenity in all
their guises; bibelots, bijou, and every kind of x-l, expendable
curios: UltraComfort™, organic skin, extendable, reversible, most
traditional kind of rubber ever, studded with tiny shards of magnetic stones. The company eventually shut down after false adver-

tising claims stuck. They "guaranteed" good health, plus the ability to heal your loved ones, through the use of magnetic holograms, which created a bridge between certain natural bodily frequencies and those in the environment. They also had the most infuriating, unforgettable jingle—it used to blare out endlessly from the tinny speakers of sales carts down by the docks, the unmistakable sound of a large corporation trying to sell tat to the needy. I don't know exactly when the miracle product began to be taken literally as some kind of fragment of god. When was it that a general alteration took place in people's prayers, and instead of asking for the Bug to go away, or for its terrible consequences to subside, people started prostrating themselves before a greater evil, one whose consequences were truly sudden and fatal: the Bug that would once and for all allow us to rest in peace? Those of us who were children in those days all had one, without exception. Birdface Helguera's stepfather worked for Mirasol, so we all got one through him. If our bracelets did engender miracles at any point, or indeed if we managed make large metal objects come toward us with a flick of the wrist, I've somehow forgotten.

41.

This: the exterminator will not succeed in eliminating rats merely by catching them. Their screeches will attract others. You have to be patient, calm the impatient body. Can you hear the way they screech? So not yet. Wait for the whole group to gather, *then* you go in. So Morgan taught me.

42.

My occasional sorties to the stationery shop are the only break in my routine. My life is not what you could call social. I worry that these deviations from my usual course will catch me away from the room, completely vulnerable. That I'll come back and find Clara sprawled on the carpet, husk-like, or like the stone of some fruit, the flesh completely devoured, and her corpse already stinking, the whole building stinking, all the buildings, the entire city, and then our neighbors will come and start asking questions, and everything will fill up with questions and muttering and sounds that are *not dissimilar from the sounds of dogs*. And there will be no way for me to explain the stone. How to tell people that in fact Clara hasn't gone but, on the contrary, she's transformed into a different kind of matter altogether, a substance somehow even more alive than you and I? They won't understand, and nothing I can do will make them. All they'll see are her dead eyes, and my dead eyes, and they'll go on looking—for answers.

43.

Dogs were the first to contract the Ź-Bug, and the earliest sign would be their fur falling out, followed within a matter of days by the claws and teeth. Soon their bones would begin to disintegrate, and within a week they would be little more than sacks of sagging skin. The response in cats was different: they could carry on as normal for quite a while. The problem came when the rats got into the grain stores, decimated them, and moved onto the mill. A new strategy had to be devised, given that starvation is well known as the best course: places in which there is an excess of foodstuff pose the greatest challenge to the exterminator. At that particular time I had been assigned a short-haired dog, half terrier, half mongrel. It had been one of the best when we were working in residential areas and stables, but at this point it became little more than useless. A meeting was called, untold options discussed, no solutions found, and it was decided, for want of any satisfactory course of action, to put the dogs back in their kennels and try something different. We returned to the mill and found the colony ten times bigger than a few days before. They had set up in the walls, the whole place was alive with the sound of them. Kovac shut his eyes and focused his attention, but his methods—poor DIY methods inside his head, little more than an attempt to rationalize what instinct was telling him—didn't help establish the movements of the colony in its current incarnation. They'd scurry out into the open, but so quickly you could be looking right at them and barely catch a glimpse, the barest trace lingering in one corner of your vision. Surplus of foodstuff: outright elimination impossible. The trick, we thought, was to put out some new kind of bait, one they hadn't gotten used to: we tried fresh offal and fish heads. We thought about it, but so did they, in their way—in their possibly far more effective way. Real intellectuals, it turned out: *they* smelled a rat, and stayed exactly where they were. Staring out at us with those little shit-injected eyes, laughing at our efforts, the stupid outfits we wore, having a right old chuckle at our tribulations, our ruined city, our call center operators doing overtime, our brethren hooked on Vakapý—staring out at us as though trying to make sense of us. What kind of creatures were we, what was up with all of these great tracts of empty space we allowed to stand between us? Anyway, we waited eight nights for the new bait to stop smelling strange to their little twitching noses. And I tried to take it easy, tried filling my mind with thoughts of the past, tried to take comfort in memories of Zulaýma. But the hours went by too slowly. Even Morgan became dejected. I initially put his quiet despondency down to the amount of time we'd spent in the company of Ź-brigadiers alone by now, or the fetid air underground, or exposure to the rat poisons. I came across him one day sitting on his own in one of the loading bays. He'd stepped out for some air but was having difficulty breathing. He said something about being lost. Being lost and not knowing how to find his way back. Something about the novice—he was talking under his breath. I swear, he said: How was I to know? He pointed a finger, then changed tack and marked an *x* in the air. There. Did you see?

Right *there*. First stop is Cambodia. And from there, on to Jakarta. We *won't* get lost . . . I had no idea what to say to any of this—I never did when Morgan started with all of that. Then the inspector gave the order to let the dogs out.

44.

Zermeño kept the best pages in his own secret pavilion of ass. No amount of jacking off could ever be worth these gals, he'd say. A special place was reserved for those topless goddesses: Zulaýma de Garay, Pita O'Higgins, Nefertiti Magaña. Zermeño wasn't much of a businessman: always getting high on his own supply. We never found out where he kept the stash but, well-hidden though it was, it became quite famous among the kids in the neighborhood, so famous that Zermeño spent great amounts of time squirreling away his goods as directed by bouts of paranoia, or motherly raids, or rumors of a supposed move by the Alanis twins and their Santa Rita underlings, a strike whose perfection was directly proportionate to its hypothetical status and was sure to strip him of his greatest treasure and his honor at the same time: those minxes with come-hither eyes and improbable contours. In his terror he also developed a steel-coated mistrust in his closest associates, us. Any time we were about to go into the ritual room (the jacking-off room) he would ask us to wait a moment. A moment that sometimes lasted several minutes. He'd bar the doors before setting up a rough and ready alarm system, dragging the bed from one side of the room to the other, slamming the wardrobes shut, opening the trunks and chests of drawers, and stacking the chairs in piles. Truth be told, I was never that interested in making off with his treasure trove. And it is the truth: people's treasure troves have simply never been of interest to me. A treasure trove is something that comes to you, but that no one ever gives you. All I was able to think about was Zulaýma, everything alfresco, her chrysalis tail enveloping me, coming down upon and around me like a mother ship: Zulaýma de Garay, owner of the biggest, firmest breasts that I have ever had the chance to imagine nibbling on: Zulaýma de Garay, née Esther Rivas Calderón, a true Atlantikan in every respect, though she did leave the city after the great affront of a silver medal in a beauty contest organized by Atlantika Telekoms, vowing never to return, only eventually doing so inside a coffin whose final destination was the bottom of the sea. But there was no way whatsoever to equate the hiding place with Zulaýma. You would have needed to be incredibly innocent to believe that those luminous breasts, with the aureole grading away gradually into the rest of the flesh, could be reduced to the two dimensions of our hurried masturbations. Zulaýma I, Empress of the Noble Empire of Jakarta, belonged to another reality altogether, a finer one, never fragile but undoubtedly delicate. This was always very clear to me, in spite of the heat and the torrent of hormones directing our every move at that time in our lives. When all was said and done, that which attracted us had very little to do with Zermeño's hiding places.

45.

My dog was in the mill for only a couple of hours. It came out with its muzzle smelling of almonds. It was the first to come back, possibly the only one. The sun was going down, Morgan was nowhere to be found, and the terrier mongrel suddenly appeared, hopping and skipping like a mad thing. Purple hops. It was purple all over: around the eyes, the nostrils, and purple the stream of mucus dribbling therefrom. It started vomiting blood. It didn't bark at all but proceeded directly to blood-streaked vomit and purple mucus. The inspector refused to waste any ammo on it. He gave me a wink. We stood and waited for the dog to die in bloody purple agony, then called the Department of Hygiene. The inspector intended to request permission to burn the building to the ground.

46.

Morgan had a notebook, and sometimes he let me look in it. He'd pretend to have left it open by accident, before disappearing off someplace. I was fairly certain I knew what this was about. We needed to empty our minds sometimes, was his view. Sluice them out, turn them upside down. Look at things another way, let it be someone else's voice claiming everything's okay. But there was more to it than that. It was his way of putting forward, in other people's words, what he himself could never say. Off he'd go, to the restroom, to stretch his legs, and there the notebook would be, miraculously open on his desk or on top of Grandma's sewing box. Too tempting. Sometimes, when I was sure he wouldn't be back for a while, I'd copy out the odd thing, sections of text that struck me as pertinent in that particular moment. This meant starting a little collection of my own, ancillary to Morgan's. I sometimes think he planned that too: that my participation, me as his copyist, was actually an important part of his plan. The original notebook had plastic covers with hemp binding and our school's emblem on the pages as a watermark. He used to steal them from the teachers' office, taking them away and filling them with material personal to him: facts that spoke to him for whatever reason, newspaper clippings, statistics, the majority of it taken from secondary sources, including at times his own dreams, I suspect. A miscellany whose provenance was impossible to establish, making my notebook like a very minor tributary to his never-ending, and in a way never-beginning, watercourse. It was his project, he used to say. He said we were welcome to spend our time gawping over unattainable females, or Vakapý, if that was our thing. Then, licking his lips with that long, sharp tongue of his, he'd dive into the pages of his notebook once more, all of those pictures and smudges, all the margins bristling with barely legible comments, the tiny letters crowding together.

47.

Zermeño's house was in the center of town, two streets from the cathedral and right across from the Galician's grocery store. The father's barbershop was part of the same property, or the barbershop was a kind of plasterboard annex tacked onto the side of the home, constantly full of the fug of rolling tobacco, his clientele's smoke of choice. Fishermen, shopkeepers, and bureaucrats alike, all whose moustaches needed seeing to first thing in the morning, or in the middle of the day, wanting a few minutes out from fish scales, tills, and ID checks, or indeed after nightfall when the freezing winds rattled in from the Atlantik, when the place became so packed that some had to stand with one foot in the room behind the annex, really only meant for customers requiring peroxide, a corrugated metal lean-to with a couple of those hairdryers that sit around your head like oversized helmets, and three pedicure stations, each with a respective pedicurist, so that on the other side of the false wall the menfolk would sit vegetating in a cloud of hair and talcum powder, flicking through the newspapers, lingering over the Page Three girls, the latest gossip about the imminent closure of the Anguja, or the Itzcuintlán Albý-Blacks' hundredth draw in a row, keeping themselves to themselves, like masculinity itself had been made manifest in the curdled smoke, all waiting their turns in the mint-colored reclinable armchairs, one of the few perks of living a life in a place where all the houses are tiny and bare. Zermeño liked to brag that his home was the greatest, the most regal, of all the houses in the center, and that if you added the barbers into the equation, theirs was the best place in all of Atlantika. And he wasn't far wrong, though it would also be correct to point out that, like almost all Atlantikan homes, the place was an unsightly monstrosity and was constantly having new bits added on and old taken off, constant architectural nips and tucks that were Zermeño's mother's weakness, in the form of ever-changing reception rooms, attics, sunrooms, porches, balconies, hallways, more hallways, always using the latest in construction technology, new high-tech insulating material, flexi-this, flush-that, flash-everything, and of course paid for by the father, poor affable Zermeño Sr., a man who would have loved nothing more than to spend his time far from the barbershop (laying a few bets) but whose conjugal commitments and inability to say no to his wife meant he spent most of it overseeing the building site or doling out cash to the construction workers.

48.

Here in the room, the stone made the dogs disappear a long time ago. But they're still around in the streets. You can hear them and they are powerful. Their barking is a way of keeping themselves company, I think, because over the course of time, with all our domestica-tory efforts, flea shampoo and flea collar and flea bait, plus just how shiny-white their canine teeth are nowadays, we've stripped man's best friend of its original resource: no longer do they howl. Simply no need. These dogs don't have a clue about running in packs, about the moon, so all you get from them is an interminable, low-level *yap yap*. They've learned to drink tea, can speak several languages, keep weekly appointments with the psychoanalyst. Then again, our ono-matopoeic *woof*, though we know it isn't always just a simple com-plaint, makes no distinction between the noise of small dogs and large. Here's a suggestion: wouldn't it be great to come up with some new terms to distinguish the alarmed bark, the don't-come-a-step-nearer bark, and the much quieter, sad, or hungry kind of bark, which is sharper, has a different tonal quality altogether, and can be like a lament and laughter at the same time? And such nomenclature would in turn require subdividing according to largeness or small-ness of dog. But if you're in the vicinity of the stone, or of Clara and the stone, the fact is they can't be heard anyway.

49.

From Morgan's notebook:

"Notes on Wellington: on occasion the copy and the original are indistinguishable. And not only that: the great copy, the perfect copy, seeks to be indistinguishable from nature, from reality, from the world."

A story: the king asks the artist to paint him a labyrinth.

50.

Sometimes, though not what you could call often, we got together at Birdface Helguera's place. His stepfather wasn't around much, and we never asked about his mother. She didn't exist. And if a thing doesn't make itself apparent, don't go digging. When Birdface wasn't around, Morgan talked about her having lain down on the train tracks when her son was very small. Morgan seemed to have this on good authority. It had fallen to Birdface's stepdad (he always referred to him as Stepdad, though not without affection), to, well, step up. He was the Mirasol man. That summer, our ninth-grade summer, they had only recently arrived—two years before, at most. Around the time the first Mirasol store opened. The factory wasn't built until a long while later, in an empty lot not far from Birdface's house. His stepdad would sometimes be gone for several days at a time, visiting the farthest corners of the state on behalf of the thriving company. Birdface told us the sales were better in those places, where his stepfather worked door to door, like in the precorporate days, all bootleggers and shoeshine guys. And so we spent quarantine-free summers—there were five decades, in all, between the Ý and the Ź. Grandma never tired of telling us how lucky we were, how blessed. But progress, hope, all of that: I never bought any of it. The only thing I felt was boredom. I sometimes wished Fish Hook's stories would come true. I wanted to know what the Bug was really like; I wanted a taste. Anything but the searing doldrums of our days, the inexorable, relentless, utterly boring passage of them. To top it off, summer was Vakapý off-season. We tattooed skulls on one another's body using compasses and Biro ink; we stole cigarettes from the grocery store and took them down to the docks to smoke. We smoked so many in such quick succession it gave us head pangs. We played tic-tac-toe with the fishermen. We went up to the freeway, Arroyo Muerto way, looking for roadkill.

51.

It's hot, and I start seeing the things I don't very often see: there, Birdface Helguera holding out a box of matches. See? In all his Birdface glory: jumpy as hell, underfed, permanent look of fright on his face. He doesn't know his time among us is short: in a few months his stepfather is going to send him to military school, and after that none of us will ever see or hear of him again. It's hot; surfaces bend and ripple in the scorching air, and there are other things the boy I then was has no way of knowing, like that Birdface and his sister take a beating just about every other day when they get home from school, and that there can be all kinds of reasons for it: because it's foggy, because their stepdad is hungry, because he's bored, and sometimes just because. There, I see it now, the mark from a belt on Birdface's forearm. A gash. A scar on his forehead. A burn on the back of his left hand. Over the years their features—eyes, mouths, noses—will warp inside my memory, change from their original composition. I now see Birdface clearly, such great clarity in the undulating particles of hot air: his body permanently trembling, his hands always ever so slightly in motion. A split-screen vision: in one of the shots, one that I can't control, can't reach in any way, he's lord and master, he rules everything there is; in the other, which shows some outside location, and the frame of which keeps pulling back, widening, I have control of the lens, and I get a view of a vacant, weed-choked lot, an uncultivated parcel of land that in later years will be the site of a mill, and after that a factory for making bracelets, home to a sect, site of a mound of dismembered pinkie fingers. The lens stops zooming out. And the land, which like us seems to cower and flinch a little, becomes a panorama comprised of objects associated with things we did when we were together: four bicycles in a pile beside the railing at the edge of the lot; a flat inner tube hanging from the branch of a tree; and nearby, a tumbledown sheet-metal hut, overrun with weeds. That was where we stored the tools, hidden under dried-out branches, and beyond it lay the area earmarked for the burn. Seen from this angle—the one arbitrarily designated to replace my real memory of the place, and one that includes features that weren't part of the original footage at all—there's an ashy cross marked in the middle of the lot. Like *x* marks the spot. Between us and the *x* stands the tongue-lolling dog we came across a few streets after setting out from the dockside market. It's having difficulty breathing, and around its neck is a leash I improvised: a twice-looped piece of rope, one end tied to a stake a little way in the distance. Usually we bring dead animals back from the freeway at Arroyo Muerto. Today Morgan decided we'd bring a live one. He's been standing there for a while, dandling a cigarette between his lips but not going so far as to light it, and not giving any of us the signal to strike a match for him either. He hasn't yet decided how to proceed. Nearby, sitting on a crate, Zermeño hurries the minutes along in the tapping of his orthopedic sandals on the ground, letting out little vexed grunts all the while: he wants recognition for having spent a large part of the morning syphoning gas from his mother's car by the old suck-on-a-hose technique. He wants Morgan to slap him on the back, wants to be appointed deputy leader. Some people are like that. Birdface, though, all he wants is to set fire to something. I see them, I see them, safety in numbers, comfort in being part of something. I see them standing beside the blurry shadows that were once my friends and that I can no longer properly make out. Morgan says something: It's the last day of summer, he says. Special occasion, special operation. To which we all nod, not expecting any response, and indeed Morgan says no more. And making no clear sign that he's noticed any of our responses in particular, he picks up his bicycle, mounts it, and cycles away. He enters a row of palm trees. One minute we can see him, the next we can't.

52.

Sometimes, when I go to the stationery shop, I try to work out which of all of those animals it was that used to wake us up at night, in the period following the Ź-Bug but before the stone's appearance in our lives. In the time before. Because it's now as though my past, the calendar in my mind, has been slashed and hacked at by some enormous blade, halved or quartered or shredded completely, and I struggle to believe in the existence of a time that fits such a description. Clara doesn't even understand the word when I say it to her. I say it over and over: *before, before, before.* She gives me the blankest look: I may as well be speaking a foreign language. Even distinguishing the two syllables, *be-fore,* comes to feel somehow pointless, though that in itself doesn't invalidate said temporal space, because for all of that, this *before* may now have become a vacant, uninhabited beginning, it did ultimately, at one point, accommodate me, and—how could it be otherwise, even me wishing it so doesn't change the fact—I do retain memories of that anterior zone: clear, fine-grained memories, close to soothing in their malleability to my mood, to the current climate. Therefore, rather than consider myself a survivor from that period of time—a period at once inexact and photographically precise—I'm better off when I go there conducting myself in the attitude of an old friend, a neighbor I once knew, say, because to go there is a comfort, and though you can make it through all kinds of horrific experiences (the tunnels, the epidemics, the rats), mangled memories are sure to be the death of anyone. Either you find a way to float above them, or, like in a sweet dream, sink down into them, but that isn't what's happening here, we aren't talking about the vacant lot itself but a vision of the vacant lot, and it's every inch as real as it seems: you can more or less do as you like there, *you* control the lens, swing the shot around like some prying neighbor, some lesser version of a busybody apartment-building dweller, the kind who loves organizing meetings for the general good of the building, opens up a bank account so everyone can pitch in for the installation of a new motor for the cistern, makes sure there's a birthday present for the porter this year. A good neighbor, the best kind: the kind who disappears without making a noise. In the lot, in the silent, weed-crazed lot, I was the best neighbor, the one who looks the other way, the one who doesn't spy, the one who makes absolutely no noise in the night. The one who suggested we start from the uninhabited beginning.

53.

The list of motivations and tools for domesticating any creature is long and varied, but at the very top is fear. Fear is a weapon that will not fail. Not pain, but rather denying any certainty about when the pain is going to end, or supplying a subtle presentiment that it may in fact never end. That it's always going to be like this. Plus the fear that you'll just get used to it, Birdface, that you'll end up needing it. A fear of the dishonesty and obscenity that follows the realization that there isn't any way to be free of the past, the realization that the pain it causes me is simply of a greater magnitude than the pain it causes you. See these marks on my skin? See what the belt has done? Well, the pain it causes me to do this to you, for all that it's invisible, is greater, is infinite, is anterior to everything. And before everything, what? More suffering. Pain begets pain; it is its own mother. But we aren't going to find this out until much later, by which time it won't matter anymore, by which time we'll have decided it's ceased to matter, or at least we'll believe it's we who've decided, as though this or any alternative were a question of deciding, purely because it won't be so distressing if we think we had a part in the decision and it won't be so distressing if nothing matters, or if it does, but only a little bit.

54.

There were mornings—I remember now—when we woke in Jakarta.

55.

It's dark by the time Morgan comes back to the lot. He has a rucksack over one shoulder and his breathing is ragged, like he's been in a chase. He doesn't apologize for having taken so long, and he doesn't need to. For Morgan, we would have waited until the end of time, or longer even: in the lot. In the lot, joined in emptiness, silent but in unison—because the stone, inscrutable as ever, stalled at that part, and because, at least in the memory, this other memory that is the stone and its visions or rather the physical sensations that the stone and its visions bring about, it may seem that in his absence there was nothing but a long silence interspersed with the first cold winds of the year, the ones that sweep down from the Sierra at nightfall to announce summer's end, unhitched convoys gusting down the slopes to crash headlong into the city, welcome, really, after the months of constant oppressive heat. That was followed by further silences, profound, harsher, or more belligerent, presaging his return. Such an interval that the dog forgot us, curled up on the ground, and slept awhile. But now Morgan's back, and the dog jumps up, as though it smells the mortal end of day, the death of day. Morgan's come a long way. He is like a heavenly body moments before it hits the earth, a comet that, after the eons of its formation, of condensing among interstellar gasses, shooting stars, water vapor, and tumultuous oxides of all kinds, is ready to take its place in the great procession—part of the code whose origin we will ultimately be forced to acknowledge as indecipherable and, what's worse, indescribable, because though the numerous obstacles that Morgan had to negotiate to arrive here do comprise an account, and though that account could well be paraphrased and examined for certain general inconsistencies, it is absurd to look for the first cause or to try to establish a schema in which earlier causes may correspond, and what's more, it is not ours to know whether what we are now seeing is but a variation: Morgan, panting, pedals into view after a period of around two hours, seeming to speed up when he senses we've seen him in the darkness, picked him out against the yellow crest-like fronds of the coastal palms (in which the rushing wind is amplified), although that shroud-like darkness, according to Clara, may be nothing more than artifice, a sham version of what was really there in the first place, so Clara says (still connected, still projecting): it's just place, an image that occupies no plane other than the general quality of place-ness, it makes very little difference who's there or what moment in time it seems to occupy, or if it happens to be another one of us, Birdface Helguera, say, emerging from the distant dark of the palm trees on a bicycle, rucksack on, for the who and the how in the rest of this story isn't the point, just as it isn't in the other stories it gives way to, that it seeds, that are its fruit, which will be nothing more than variations on older refrains, ballad-like repetitions forged out of the tiniest errors, a concatenation of smallest departures from the truth: these will have been altered in advance and spring from another beginning that, unimaginable though it is to us, we posit as a given: each version, notwithstanding the apparent likenesses, is independent of all the others and would appear different, there would be differences between the notional plants in those backgrounds and the ones in front of which Morgan now stops, laying the bicycle down and coming toward us: we ourselves are crisscrossed by so many forks in the path: there are vacant weedy lots that are people's lives: there are lives that are the evergreens, because none of the flora here in Atlantika grows upward via rigid stems, because they are all pretense, are all perfectly *flexible,* all composed of filaments, strands, fibers, all subsumed within a mysterious system through which the vital sap courses, flooding and eventually breaking each and every one of them down. In the end it doesn't matter who is Morgan: we are all bound by so, so many commissures, all driven on by the grinding of teeth. The big thick thing that is a tongue. I smile at them. I remember who I am. The rest of the boys glance nervously at one another and then I, with a slight wave of my hand, announce that it's time.

56.

The upper part of the plain that we had crossed the day before was now red with snow, and it was evident that there was a storm raging behind us and that we had only just crossed the Burji La in time to escape it. We camped in a slight hollow at Sekbachan, eighteen miles from Malik Mar, the night as still as the previous one and the temperature the same; it seemed as if the Deosai Plains were not going to be so formidable as they had been described; but the third day a storm of hail, sleet, and snow alternately came at noon when we began to ascend the Sari Sangar Pass, 14,200 feet, and continued with only a few minutes' intermission till four o'clock. The top of the pass is a fairly level valley containing two lakes, their shores formed of boulders that seemed impossible to ride over. The men slid and stumbled so much that I would not let anyone lead my pony for fear of pulling him over; he was old and slow but perfectly splendid here, picking his way among the rocks without a falter. At the summit there is a cairn on which each man threw a stone, and here it is customary to give payment to the coolies. I paid each man his agreed-upon wage, and, alone, began the descent. Ahead was Jakarta.

57.

We gather newspaper and twigs from the hut and make a bundle. I carry the demijohn over to the ashy mound, though it's Zermeño who takes the cap off and pours out a little of the gasoline. Birdface has lit a match. He holds it between forefinger and thumb. The flame seems not to move down the match but to remain burning just at the tip. The dog, terrified by the blaze, backs away as far as the rope will allow. The fire gives off a dirty, foul-smelling smoke. Beyond the smoke and the heat I can see Birdface: he's smiling, or trying to smile, his stubby canines flat as molars. We turn and see Morgan bending slowly down, moving in skidding slow-motion. Then, arching his back, he comes to crouching and reaches into his rucksack, reaches deep inside: in this movement, I now see, lies the trick, the assiduously careless gesture of the magician: his hand moves, and, just as it falls on the thing it's looking for, it stops, renouncing the quest: his forefinger and thumb are no longer apparent as they yank open the zipper, nor as the triumphant pincer brings forth the gun. Only his hands, in motion. It's my pop's, says Morgan, he keeps it in case of burglaries. There is a kind of aural residue to his voice, a second voice carried on the wind, nearly evaporating before it reaches us though, in fact, it will never evaporate. A voice I remember. In the firelight, shadows dance across our faces, and we look younger than we are. I can see it: we look almost like children. Morgan says otherwise: we're grown-ups now, according to him. The voice bleeds into everything, like a thick ubiquitous film that spreads and dries in an instant, possibly on account of the wind or possibly on account of its own chemical makeup: dry and static, forming a kind of exoskeleton for the railing, the dog, the flames, the rucksack: only the hands move, and that faster and faster, because everything else seems to have acquired a thick, glaze-like coating under the second voice, us included, frowning adults, adults-in-waiting, undefined, perching on the very cusp of past and present. Right here, says Morgan, right now. We each nod. He raises the gun and, one by one, points it at each of us. When it comes to me, when I'm looking down the barrel—and see beyond it Morgan's eye—my legs go numb. Morgan laughs; Zermeño laughs too, but nervously. Zermeño, those deep-set, bloodshot eyes of his. He's going to be a barber like his father, and like his father's father before, like his sons, grandchildren, all Zermeño progeny. He ought to know, and we do at that point all know it, but Zermeño himself, there in the interzone of adolescence, his face awash with zits, still labors under the illusion that one day he'll be somebody. Like a politician. Not that cutting people's hair isn't an estimable thing to do. Or doing the shampoo, or the part when they get rid of the hair around your collar with one of those brushes dipped in talcum powder. The problem is Zermeño, his infinite sense of shame, his desire to be something. Look at him now. That laugh: pure fear. The laughter of pure cowardice, like glass shattering. The safety's on, you fag, says Morgan, teeth ever so slightly angled back in his mouth on account of his constantly pulling them back in with the tip of his tongue, that pleased, pleasurable look that comes over his face when the rest of us show any sign of fear. He spins the chamber and points the gun straight up at the sky. He holds the gun like Flash Gordon. Flipping open the chamber, he shows us the three bullets. The kickback is a bitch, I hear him say. Where'd you learn to shoot? says Zermeño. My pop. It's easy, just like in the movies. Just gotta be ready for the recoil, you can lose a tooth. Gotta grip the hilt good. What's the hilt? someone asks, maybe me. This bit here, fag. Then the gun is in my hands. My finger cradled snugly by the trigger. My knees hip-width apart. Braced. Good. It's heavy in my hand, and cold. Black. A very sort of black. The blackest black I've ever seen. We're grown-ups now, Morgan says again, winking at me.

58.

From Morgan's notebook:

"Our Lady of the Chrysalids healing lepers, photocopy of original manuscript: Gospel of Federico the Moor.

Emperor Obdulio as a leper, reproduction of fresco: Chapel of Saint
Atillus.

Saint Damian distributing alms among poor and sick, copy on canvas of original on slate.

Our Lady of the Chrysalids with trio of beggars. Attributed to Holbein
the Elder. Lithograph??"

59.

We didn't bury it but we made sure not to use up all the gasoline
either. Let's save some, said Morgan, for when we find more. More
what? More animals, fag. We placed what remained of the carcass
in a plastic bag and left it in a corner of the lot. Every day I'd take a
detour on my way home from school to go and have a look: lots of
flies at first, then fewer. It shrank in size, became progressively paler.
And one day disappeared completely.

60.

That was our last year at school. A year of quiet. Even the old nun
didn't say much. She had a hip problem and would fall asleep halfway through class and wake with a start at the sound of the buzzer;
she was so close to being dead she reminded us of a stuffed animal. I
remember one time when she started nodding off and Birdface tore
all the pages out of his notebooks, put them in a wastepaper basket
next to the bookshelves and put a match to them. Everyone jumped
up and started running about, kicking things over, until soon the
room was thick with smoke. At first we thought the nun hadn't noticed
because she was so out of it: a stuffed owl, her false teeth hanging
half out of her mouth. In fact she was awake the entire time, even

as the flames began to lick her wooden chair. A couple of boys with sleepy faces got up and dragged her out of the classroom. The fire alarms went off and the school was evacuated. We spent that afternoon playing football in a field out back of school. Next day, as soon as we arrived at school, the Mother Superior made us all line up in the yard. The nun had been admitted to one of the charity's clinics—in a state of shock, the Mother Superior said, as if we cared. As punishment, and until the guilty party owned up, we were all given detention in the shape of having to stand out by the flagpole from seven in the morning until two in the afternoon, two whole weeks outside in the blistering sun, and given nothing to eat until one of our number wilted—a little pansy fag bitch of the kind that proliferate in prisons for impoverished children (which was what our school was), one of the ones who become sponges for everyone else's anger, especially when we caught a glimpse of the men the pansy fag bitches were going to become, and in that saw more clearly the malignant beings *we* were going to become and whom time and boredom would make only more malignant: the wilting little pussy Neto, poor fucker, who at some point passed out. Fine. He wilted. The problem was that Fatty Muñoz broke too, moved by the sight of Neto hitting the ground but mainly moved by the pangs in his empty stomach, and, tears streaming down his face, gave Birdface up. After that the novice was never spoken of again. It was like she ceased to exist. Birdface was expelled, and that was the last we officially heard of him as well, though the rumor about the provincial military school did gain currency. Morgan said we were all morons. Birdface's stepfather knew about the novice, he said, and to prevent police involvement, he'd requested a transfer and slung Birdface in a mental hospital for good measure. Not just that, but it was the stepfather himself who'd started the military school rumor, as a way of protecting his name—his and that of Mirasol. None of us believed a word of this. Morgan was forever making things up, convincing himself of the truth of his tales. We were playing tetherball one afternoon when he came up with a plan to break Birdface out. He'd established his whereabouts, an institution

on the outskirts of the city, on the Dos Bocas road. We just needed
to do exactly as he said (of course): set up a rotation for each of us to
go over there on weekends and get friendly with the guards, who did
eight-hour shifts on Saturdays and twelve-hour shifts on Sundays.
The hard part would be getting inside; for that we'd need to create a distraction. That's where Zermeño would come in. Then what?
None of us knew how to drive, and Morgan, after obsessing over the
plan for a while, simply forgot all about it. As for Fatty M, poor, poor
fucker, he started catching a beating every single recess for the rest
of that school year. Then he moved schools as well. The nun came
back to work a few days after the incident, and that was also when
she stopped with the recital of foreign capitals. The register became a
numbered list like in everyone else's classes; in places like our school
nobody ever learns your name. You're a number, a capital city if you're
lucky. I was almost always Jakarta, but I don't remember the number I
was then given. In any case, the new dispensation didn't last long. The
nun hung on till the end of that school year then died.

61.

I bet on Vakapý and Clara makes guesses over the date when the
stone may have landed on earth. There's no great difference, she says,
between such numbers games and the extinction of the world as we
know it. I disagree. For starters, Vakapý is more than just a numbers
game. Yes, it can be boiled down to the flight of the ball throughout each match, a series of trajectories that in turn may be made
into a series of digits, which in turn may be stored and interpreted
in such a way as to expand a database whose function is to regulate
and administer the prices that then dictate the gamblers' moves, but
there are so many other factors that the overall mathematics of the
game depend upon, factors that in turn depend upon mathematics in order to affect the game. Plus, the fact that we survived the
epidemics suggests we are condemned to stick around—against all

odds, against all prognostications—though not in perpetuity. The stone will outlive us all. Of this she is convinced, pointing to many ancient manuscripts that support the idea. The Fifth Sun of the Mayans. Small explosions. Cosmic radiation. Electromagnetic phenomena. The stone is merely material evidence of her theory. She's written out the equation for me with her finger in the air many times. Don't you see, she says? So simple, so devastatingly simple: assign a value to each object in the room. Whatever happens to be in the room. Now, if we could focus our attention on each of the elements comprising this small space, she says, distributing our focus across each little thing in equal measure, each would necessarily decompose—in the mathematical sense, separate into simpler constituents—and these in turn would demand closer, or deeper, inspection. And each could in turn be broken down in a succession that would lead to the ultimate clarification or illumination. Like little boxes, one inside the other. And would some vestige remain, some cipher at least? The remainder I have already synthesized, she says, pointing at the red and blue dots she's been painting on the walls these past months. See? She believes that the end will come in the shape of a stone identical to hers, only larger. I've tried to make the counter case: that it's impossible to establish an end for the same reason it's impossible to know the nature of the beginning, that the end will not be a thing to fit in words, or stones, or numbers, that the end is not ours to know, and that should such a time come when we are able to name it, that will be the very moment in which our powers of description fail, break down, in every sense decompose. We will have become dust, or a vase, or the distant sound of barking. This is what dust is: all that is yet to be. That was my thought, and I told Clara. She giggled. I spent nights unable to sleep, observing her. I've now become certain that the end will come from within. Even an earthquake is a matter of a body—the continent—contracting, pushing down on itself, disappearing into itself . . . And yet it is an earthquake, something we can name. There are even instruments for measuring it, and a specific measure for quantifying those tektonik shudders.

62.

There weren't any more animals. We never went back to the lot.

63.

"Many different aboriginal cultures held that it was in the bones that the vital energy lay. Bones are the toughest, longest-lasting parts of the body. Flesh and blood are the houses for soul and spirit, but they are essentially volatile, and may and do pass away. Whereas the soul contained in bones *transmutes*. —R. Velásquez

Who saved the world in '58? Who were the heroes? It sure as hell wasn't any of us."

64.

In order to become a master carpenter what you need are patience and years of practice. Certain skills can be acquired only over time. For example, the rosewoods native to this region, in spite of their apparent hardiness, can very easily split from within and must be handled with utmost care. All the kind of rowan one finds on the islands, unlike the European varieties, have barely any sapwood and can therefore be polished almost endlessly. It's usual to lose a certain amount of volume when you come to plane the wood—sometimes as much as four to eight centimeters—which is why a good grasp of your materials is essential. Whether because we couldn't be bothered or because we were cursed, it didn't matter, we regularly got it wrong, and any materials we squandered out of cack-handedness or simple negligence—again the end result was the same—was taken out of our wages. To say we weren't cut out for the job would be about right, and no amount of sawdust in our hair or splinters in our fingers could hide the fact. We weren't hugely taken by the prospect of the kind of work that meant being shut inside, particularly in the summer months, sawing, planing, and sanding furniture for other people to relax on, drinking the kinds of cold beers we'd never be able to afford. And so our inauspicious carpentry careers ended before they had begun, specifically on the day Morgan had the bright idea of plundering the workshop, a workshop in which we would later meet again, quite by coincidence—or very nearly by coincidence. Four years is a long time. A very long time, at that point. A fifth of our lives to date, a succession of days and nights whose forward march had been interrupted only by sleep, vacations, our games of arson, games of Vakapý, or the discovery of those 2-D female forms to which we commended our astonished semen. Similarly it takes time to learn the trick of scavenging your past for details, though one can never become a master in it. Possibly I wasn't always interested in doing so; imagining the incomplete future kept me more than busy enough. Nowadays, though, I stockpile the details that seem to me equivocal, ambiguous, the conjectural and the open to discussion, moments that I have learned to look upon as part of an interminable network of variations or even variability, the bone house of memory— directly adjacent to the mound of rotting corpses, the arms, fingers, legs, and heads. It certainly came in handy in the Ź-Brigades. People I had known. Fatty Muñoz, for example, I thought of him: had I really known him? We'd been in the same class for the entirety of my school career, and I never knew anything about his life. He was just a punching bag, even for the most cowardly among us, even for the puniest little bastards—for the cowards and the puny bastards especially, those of us who inflicted pain on others so that no one else would inflict pain on us. Suffering is a kind of mother tongue, an umbilical cord with our own humanity: if you've hurt someone, or in the moments when you yourself are being hurt, you're not alone. I suppose the opposite also holds: there's company in castigation, but the tension that constitutes pain can also suspend it, bringing in a harsher kind of emptiness still, plunging you into a void that is even less traversable. A feeling that is liable to go on for months, years even, incubating inside you. Strange to think how we all eventually disappear, and how our place is in a sense taken by other people's diffuse memories of us. A shadow of the pain. Because one day people cease to exist. We ourselves cease to exist, we vacate ourselves. So: Morgan quit school and went off to become a boxer. He had no more time for pussies like us anymore; his new cohorts were older, bigger, and way more streetwise. At some point we saw his name on a poster in the Talabarteros truck terminal; it turned out he'd been training at a gym on Cordillera Hill and was now down to take part in a night featuring twenty separate bouts, making him one of forty guys wearing boxing gloves that were complete strangers to us. After that he vanished. Zermeño was the last to go. He took up the family trade, had no more time for teen pranks and foolishness. So it goes. I went down to the docks on my own. I stole from Grandma, I sold this and that, bought this and that. Same as ever. As it turned out, life without Morgan was also a kind of life.

65.

From the notebook:

"The old coat of arms for the Noble Empire of Jakarta, used during the days of the Vice Royalty, comprises two scenes: the first, in the upper panel, depicts Our Lady of the Chrysalids, wellspring of all Reason and Justice, with right hand extended in blessing of a man whose skin is covered in welts and sores. He has a horn attached to his back to announce his affliction. Then, in the lower panel, we see him cured, smiling, dressed in new clothes: postmiracle. He's holding a stone, dark in color, gleaming, and the size of an Adam's apple: a postal vote for the Virgin, perhaps, or an offering. In the back ground, beaming with emotion, stand a farmer and his wife, and a pair of sheep. The representation of Our Lady of the Chrysalids, with her virtue manifest in a pupae halo and the clasped hands of prayer, is the same posture of mercy all the great masters opted for."

66.

Morgan. Morgan. Morgan. It wasn't in the carpentry workshop that we saw each other next, but in the queue at the military recruitment office. His dandruff mixing with mine. Or so it might have been, were it not for the fact his buzz cut and new nose (flat as a pancake) meant I barely noticed whether any scaly dead skin adorned his head. And actually I didn't recognize him at first; but he recognized me, and a smile instantly bloomed on his face. I stepped back and took him in properly, and what a sight: he was cadaverously thin, with a taut covering of skin stretched across his bones, and that was about all. He was holding a vaccination card and, in the same hand, a transparent baggy containing the passport photos stipulated by the recruitment office for the paperwork. He held out the other to shake. A tentacle, I thought. I found it difficult to believe it when he said he'd carried on boxing.

67.

We were queue mates till we got to the front and had to hand over the documents to the officer, along with our birth certificates, the photos, and a couple of pieces of paper with stamps from other less important but equally inefficient official bodies. This was still in the days when it was forbidden to go walking around in public like the unfortunate souls of the very early phases of the Ź-Bug— unfortunate, stupid, or convinced this was the only patriotic thing to do. It was summer (just like it is now). There was public dismay at the widespread flooding and the utter uselessness of the drainage efforts. The devout were gearing up for spawning season at the

Saint Bartolo pools. Akuâ II had just broken the record for matches unbeaten at the new Vakapý courts. The Žocalo was being occupied in protest at the closure of the Anguĵa. Those days. Documents duly handed over, as Morgan and I left I realized how little we had spoken in the two hours together. Our shared past aside, there was nothing to distinguish us from that miserable peloton of acne-covered losers. We'd never talked much anyway, it then struck me. I wanted to tell him about the dog, about the way it had shrunk so gradually and eventually faded to nothing; I wanted to know if he'd gone to look at that carcass turned fly swarm turned void as well. I wanted to talk about the novice. But at the same time, I wanted to watch him walk off and never come back. We waited outside the office as the draw was prepared, leaning against a wall on which a mural read, "The astronomers were wrong." A couple of cigarettes later we were called inside, and we both pulled black balls out of the hat: it was the reserves for us; they'd call us. As we went to leave, just as I was getting ready to be alone once more, to vanish, to go back to happily keeping myself to myself, Morgan told me about a fight he was taking part in on the outskirts. He said I should come along.

68.

All I can recall of the following week is a pain suddenly springing up in my chest and trying to conjure an excuse. Really, there were more than enough excuses I could have used, I was just too much of a coward to put any forward. Perceiving the outline of your fear is one thing, doing something about it quite another. I wrestled with the idea, hardly able to sleep: the days slipped by, and the nights, and as Wednesday turned to Thursday I finally plummeted into deepest sleep. It was after midday when eventually I awoke, and I spent the rest of the afternoon sitting on a bench in Parque Progreso. Later, home once more, I stepped into the shower and, standing beneath the cold stream, succeeded in condensing the anxiety, depositing it in a single point up on the green grouting between the bathroom tiles. The pieces inside my head, placed side by side with the patchwork puzzle of limescale and damp-riddled corners, finally seemed to fit. He'd come back, Morgan. Like an apparition. The unease that had taken up residence in my solar plexus abated, to be replaced by the low-level bodily memory that amputees say takes up residence following the loss of a limb: a dropped-ballast sensation, yet one of such pressing urgency that it then becomes impossible to suppress the tingling, prickly feeling, confirmation that where once there was a weight there is now only this empty nothing; but what's worse, this confirmation, as it were, not of the loss but rather of the former possession, manifested too late in the spiritual baggage of my adulthood, because having lost part of something I hadn't been aware of, I could now see that it was only a matter of time before the body, my clearly autonomous anatomy, once more became accustomed to the presence of this now intermittent pinprick that was Morgan— that Morgan the pinprick, the previously unappreciated prosthesis in my existence, was going to become a given in my life once more. I went and got on the bus, preoccupied with the heavy feeling a prosthesis projects into the contiguous zone where once there was (and is now!) flesh and bone (a *meaty* void), a force I thought had been buried, the sensation of another time, nagging, a bitter tinge to your gums, spreading to your throat and nasal cavity . . . The bus driver was playing a disk of old dance numbers, the kind Grandma used to love. Have I talked about her? Oh, probably. She could be another beginning—a whole territory of other beginnings. At around nine that evening I got off the bus outside the stadium. The bus had taken just about the most circuitous route possible, though it's quite possible that I knew it was going to do so, which at least meant I could skip the undercard. I've never liked boxing. To me it's like the antithesis of Vakapý, no other aspiration than to be a weary fuck-you to any and all interpretations by intellectuals, and by unintellectuals, and by everyone in between, a pastime utterly resistant to being anything other than what it simply is: a couple of brutes punching each other in the heads for the entertainment of another set of brutes who, unlike them, have money. And yet this clear memory: the sensation that came over me as the first bell rang, one that I'm certain had nothing to do with my own blood rising. It came from some far-off place, some isolated locale, fleshless, a-visceral. Morgan's fight was one of several, of numerous different weight classifications, on the evening's interminable card. And yet, and yet, the lights looked different when it came to him. The lighting, which until then had been a mad latticework of roving spotlights, now gave way to a strobe sequence. Morgan was the first of the duo to emerge, flanked by a trio of underfed cheerleaders, his trainer, and the guy with the ice bucket. The sequins on his shorts were pale blue, matching his boots, which had similarly shiny tassels and two-tone laces. The emcee, in tones as vain as his hairpiece, announced the boxers' respective weights, reaches, and records. *Clang, clang, clang*, went the bell, and within a couple of minutes Morgan was stumbling into the ropes, his face a bloody mess. And me? I tried to hide my smile. Was this it, had I found happiness? This dropping sensation in the pit of my stomach, so similar to a settling of scores. There, among the braying public, the lights, the haze of cigarette smoke, the drink and snack vendors, a combination that in my mind represented the lowest echelon of human existence: there I suddenly found contentment, a sense of completion, while at the same time feeling somewhat for the recipient of that awful blood-shower of a beating. Not in eight rounds did he lay a glove on his opponent, a wiry black guy from Dos Bocas with abnormally long arms and an alarmingly low center of gravity. He took three steps to every one of Morgan's; he feinted, danced, and mixed jabs and hooks such that Morgan looked at least a hundred pounds the heavier. I ought still to point out that in spite of all, Morgan never threw in the towel, and he didn't hit the canvas once. Round eight, the ref stopped the carnage. Morgan, his legs completely gone, carried on swinging at thin air in slow motion, his manager and the ref keeping him upright as best they could. He looked desperately out into the crowd, trying to identify an imaginary opponent, but somehow his gaze slipped straight across me. That evening was the end of his time as a boxer, W3-L14, and it was back to days and nights down at the docks for us. Our old carpentry teacher got us apprentice positions in a workshop not far from the docks. The pay was terrible, but still it was hardly the worst job, basically goofing most of the day away, plus we made a little on the side selling sawdust to a local chinchilla breeder. But then Morgan set his eye on a table saw and a semifixed router and roped me in to helping steal them one night after closing time. The owner didn't even bother to investigate: we were both sacked the next day. Morgan had found buyers beforehand, and we split the profit, which it took us less than a week to spend. Not long after that, the bodies of the first children were found down by the canal. The Department of Hygiene announced a massive recruitment drive: if you were young, had finished school, were looking for a competitive salary and the opportunity to take your career in public health to the next level, you should get in touch.

69.

I had lots of siblings, then not so many. Like any good Chrysalid devotee, Grandma spawned every five years on the dot. They were more or less like shadows in my life, most of them gone before I had a chance to meet them. Those who stuck around soon started making themselves scarce. They left their vaccination cards in a box along with the odd shoe. We lived off handouts, it's true, but a better sort of handout, never having to resort to shoelace stew or any other abject practice of the truly desperate. Grandma did her best, also true, and yet they all left her in the end. She made sure we had the basics of Vakapý, got us on the charity's books, saw that our childhoods were overseen by nuns and monks: that was how you made good men, good citizens. And out of nothing, as though fermented by the absence of air and the heat given off by the electrical resistors, made they were. Before leaving school, several of my siblings already had kiosk jobs lined up. One of my many brothers (too many to count) even rose to become a councilor on a cross-party ticket in one of the towns on the border. It was in the paper. Our neighbors brought Grandma a garland of lilies in recognition of her formative role. An afternoon of songs and festivities, and a suckling pig slaughtered. We got to take the leftovers home (snout and cheeks), and those rounds of applause rang in our ears for quite some time. We are the prosperous types, as anyone can see: we come from good stock, for all that paltry ambition plagues us. All my other brothers and sisters felt the call of success and one by one cleared out, until it was just me and Grandma. We never saw any of them again. I personally never learned the knack of missing them, unlike Grandma, who sometimes took out their old IDs and vaccination cards, proof of our immunity to polio and other ills, which she would caress and coo over for a while. I was the last of her spawn; after I came along, she attended church only for services. I always somehow knew that, unlike the others, I was destined to stick around.

70.

At that time I was getting up more or less with the fishermen, taking a bus to HQ, putting on the hazmat suit, and heading underground. It had ceased to be a question of simply piling up the bodies and burning infected buildings. In its second phase, the job consisted of clearing the tunnels of rats, eliminating them. In and out: quick as you like. Except . . . the problem, they said, was that the creatures had taken up home in the pipes along which the telephone wires were laid. This was much worse than having to sand vast pieces of wood at the workshop, not only because of the ridiculousness of saving telephone wires in a deserted city where nobody was going to be calling anybody, but also because tight spaces become even more cramped if you throw infectious disease into the mix. Pest control on this scale is a question of patience: you install the traps and the poison, and you wait. You learn a few tricks along the way. Like fumigating the traps, smudging them with a brush dipped in something like aniseed oil, for instance, to take away the smell of humans. But the fundamental thing is patience. You have to know how to wait if you're going to become a genuine exterminator. Down in the tunnels, time becomes a burden. In the dark, when all is silent, we could tell how numerous a colony was from the scratching and scuffling of their claws farther along the pipes. Morgan and I could spend up to twelve hours at a time beneath the earth, putting out traps, swimming around in shit.

71.

No other country in the world distributes its centers of power across three different cities, said Morgan. So, like, South Africa, that's probably ginormous, right? And so you've got to be thinking about a pretty tight system of governance: big country, varied vegetation, all kinds of different animals, you just can't run that kind of show without *efficiency*. As we waited in the darkness, our minds filled with South Africa, its hypothetical immensity: a ripe medley of ideas, species, moods, and creatures. Meanwhile we were tuning in to the presence of the rats, honing our senses to be more like Kovac's, trying to detect the slightest alterations in their emanations. We split the shifts up between three of us, taking it in turns to be on watch: sometimes when a colony was cornered, the rats would rush en masse to a different sector seemingly at random, obeying the dictates of an intelligence beyond us, a collective animus that also signified the Ź-Bug's terminal phase. They knew they had numerical advantage, and down came the avalanche. Nothing for it but to hit the deck facedown, just let them roll over us. Pretoria, Cape Town, Bloemfontein. They'd take little nibbles of the hazmat

suits as they went by: the teeth scraping the breathing apparatus, those long claws, and those eyes, thousands of eyes, which in
the light of the dark lantern had the appearance of multicolored
sequins. When it rained, the tunnels would flood, and a good number of them would be washed away—all the worse for us, since we'd
be sent to unclog the hatchways. We took the carcasses to the lab-
oratory, where the bacteriologists analyzed the swollen teats in an
attempt to establish how advanced the Ž-Bug was. But for all the
scientists' efforts to classify the situation, they were a long way from
having a handle on it. Nobody was thinking about the next day, or
the one after that. Above us, on ground level, the new recruits were
being sent out to count the dead, while in the universities, valu-
able resources were being squandered in the desperate attempt to
draw conclusions. We went on filling our leather sacks with dead
rats, taking them back to HQ, and rinsing them with oxygen-
ated water and chlorine. We were paid per head. The Department
pointed to this as a way of encouraging competitiveness—as necessary in the overall fight for survival, if not more, than the science—
though it was also good for morale. But the Atlantikans up above,
those hazy figures who were supposed to motivate us to spend days
and nights swimming around in rodent excrement, trying to turn
up the swollen teats of the zero agent, had mostly abandoned the
city or expired, and those who remained were close to death, hud-
dling together inside the overcrowded warehouses provided by the
Department of Hygiene (buildings without running water, light,
or medicine), lying on cots that at points in the epidemic had to
be shared between two or three people. But none of that was our
concern. We just focused on bringing in the carcasses. Once, 50 of
them came tumbling out of my sack at the end of a shift. That's a
decent shift. I read somewhere that an exterminator in China did
40,000 rats in a single year—about 110 a day. There are all kinds of
strange people in China; apparently they even eat rats. Fine, I say,
you can have rat soup, have whatever you want, but those kinds of
figures are truly insane.

72.

We've spent all evening connected to the stone. The images are of my time in school. Some days they pertain to the origin of the Bug, others to my time in the tunnels. As for Jakarta, I go there alone: crossing wide valleys and, at the end, scaling the peak. The ascent is not easy. Most of the time the two cities, Atlantika and Jakarta, meld together in a ragged, overlapping confusion of sights and sounds. I go back to bed, stretch out my arms and legs. The fan keeps turning. The nun, wrinkle on wrinkle, calls out the register. Jakarta is almost worn out, worn to near invisibility, from all the folding and refolding of her sheet of paper. Ours is a school for the poor, by the poor: the source of all poverty. We don't even have a globe: the world is revealed to us in each lesson when the nun brings out a rectangular piece of paper. Carefully rolling it out and pinning it up on a corkboard, she stands next to it, very still, like the confounded navigator at the edge of the flat, known world. One of the children, maybe Morgan, never being one for souls (but apparitions, yes, very much so), asked with a laugh whether the novice's soul might be wandering around in the school, over the bumpy flagstones of the yard, past the tetherball post and the mini Vakapý court with its faded boundaries, the restrooms, the communal shop, the parent room, or even across this cheap print of the world with its incorrect scaling, all the coasts too long or too short: see, there's our country, its dotted edges intended to correspond in some way with the realm we inhabit: It's shaped like a horn, you say, a horn of great abundance, a cornucopia, you cry, whereas what I see is nothing less than a pistol, and not just me, we all think it's like a gun, because that clearly is what it's like, and not a horn full to the brim with tasty morsels: see, says Morgan, there's the barrel, there's the sights, there's the black chamber, and I'd say the novice, dead or alive, could easily live in a ghost country such as that. But his voice cracks as he says this, he's gasping, tears are running down Morgan's face. The whole class looks round, incredulous. Or maybe it was me who put this to the nun, and Morgan was crying all along. Nobody knows what's happening except that he's crying, crying, the room fills with the sound of Morgan's lament. The nun, impassive, says that such passing concerns are of little matter in questions of the soul: in metaphysical terms, political divisions and their cartographic representations are really all one. And is there, in the end, any difference? Maybe the falsehood lies not in representation itself but in the very thing we seek to represent when we resort to down or upscaling, to euphemism. Because as it happens this country isn't real, nor has it ever been: it is a thing barely intuited, like a compilation of familiar imprecisions, like those that filter down to us through dreams: faces, smells, landscapes. The similarities between the countries on the map and the countries on earth are so great, by dint of existing in name only, that at times one has little choice but to ask: Which of the two do we inhabit and when did we cross the line? We jump from one to the other constantly, hardly noticing the borders that separate them. But to the souls of men and women, such things are not a concern. If the flesh is incapable of keeping them prisoner, why should concrete or granite be able to? This is a point on which the nun will not be swayed. She moves on to talk of immortality, and the means for attaining it, as though running us through a recipe for chicken pie. It's hot: the blades of the fan, or just one single blade, flying around, infinite. I see my hands. The trembling dog outside the mill, up on Cordillera Hill, next to the dump: barking and vomiting and maybe also yawning, all at the same time. My hands are trembling too. The fan blades, overlapping, moving mandala-like. I remember that dogs keep themselves cool through the pads of their paws—this is known as evolution, I remember. I shut my eyes. The fan rumbles on.

73.

Grandma wasn't buried and I didn't let anyone cremate her either. I didn't eat her remains. Nobody did. Though I never shared her faith, that would have been sacrilege, unacceptable. She manufactured a plastic bag for herself, climbed inside it, and waited for the end to come. We took her out to the lot and propped her up in one corner. I went by every day on my way home from Ź-Brigade work: the puparium gradually diminishing, its color fading. Then one day they all hatched. Then there was nothing left.

74.

The plan now is to test the precise effect the heat has on the visions. Cases of Ź-Bug were spiraling, the hospitals were turning people away. The quarantine was announced: the Department of Hygiene had no choice. At the same time buildings were evacuated and droves fled the city. The Ź-Brigades did not emerge unscathed, far from it: the infection was perfectly happy to follow us underground, and after six months, between desertions and deaths, we'd lost at least a hundred of our comrades. Even the ones who had shown courage and/or bravery, the psychos or those with no family and nothing else to lose either, began trickling away once we passed the ninety-day mark. Everyone feared infection. The fear got worse at night. One of the exterminators, a Sierra boy who kept to himself (and whom I therefore liked), would check his room ten times before getting into bed. Only once he'd peered into each and every cranny, all the air vents and even the power sockets, would he consent to lie down and sleep. All of which was pointless: someone would always start coughing in the night, or you'd hear the sound of retching in one of the rooms. You'd turn over in bed and lie listening to the shifting bodies, the creaking springs, the grinding of teeth. Your mind full of the toxins drifting around on the air. Every morning when the alarm went, we'd get up bleary-eyed, hardly having slept, legs aching from dragging the weight of those hazmat suits around. I believe Morgan was the only reason I survived the tunnels. It felt like wallowing in a mud trap, like we were slowly, slowly being submerged, and there would be no other end to it. One day our captain set the alarm even earlier than usual: Right, boys, he said, it's the front line for us. Get your things; we're heading to the earth's core. It was then that the tunnel came crashing down on top of us.

75.

From the notebook:

"Our design for the lift tower left us with a vast blind wall of in situ concrete. There was thus the danger of having a dreary expanse of blankness in that immensely important part of the building. A solution had to be found. The great wall space would provide an opportunity for a gesture of thanks to the people of Jakarta; a stone would be placed in front of it. And, instead of standing in the shadows, the Stele of the Measures would be brought there also. The wall would be divided, by means of softly worn paths, into doors. These, varying in size from the very large to the very small, would have different colors and thicknesses. Some would open, some would not, and this would change from week to week, or from hour to hour, or in accord with sounds made by people standing in front of them. Long lines or tracks would run from the doors into the roaring public spaces."

76.

The stone shows us a very clear picture of a night when the exterminator from the Sierra took a screwdriver and tore off his own fingernails, having become convinced the Ź-Bug, in defiance of his security measures, had taken up residence underneath them. He spent the next couple of days with his hands in bandages, howling in the infirmary after mealtimes. Then back to work. Hey, you guys, he said. Hey, Atlantikans, I saved your lives. Right? I saved your goddamn lives. Laughter from all of us.

77.

People want to know about the explosion. What gave way first, they want to know: our sense of hearing or our sense of sight? Or both at once? Or did one go and pull the other down after it, like in an avalanche when the snow plummets down the mountainside, effectively becoming frost, wind, and rain at the same time? In fact snow is appropriate in a way: the way it is prone to avalanches, and its redness. Blindness is by all accounts a redness: a snowy expanse, no horizon. What, they say, so the noise came, and then you couldn't see? The back of the skull picked up the rumble before any other part of you? All right, okay, fine: after being given the all clear by the medics, Morgan was put before a Brigade tribunal. The only answer he gave his interrogators was to repeat the same story he'd told us in the tunnels a few days earlier, concerning a clutch of lark eggs, the sun, and a herd of cattle that briefly stopped chewing their cud. The story had nothing in it about any human beings. A large number of rats died, more rats than men, it's true. That was what he said. He said nothing about the explosion, not what it was like, nothing about the gunpowder smell that accompanied it or the packed earth that came pouring down on our heads. Those eggs, on the other hand, he described in loving detail: completely intact, and dun brown with little wisps of a darker brown flecking the surface. The tribunal ordered him to be discharged, stating probable brain injury. They never once considered the possibility that Morgan was having them on. It could also have been one in an endless series of explosions, *a series with neither beginning nor end,* or just as possibly a one-of-a-kind tremor, utterly uniform everywhere it was heard because it never encountered any obstacles: this was part of my opening statement when I was called. The first thing was the absence of sound, next a shrill buzzing in our eardrums, a tiny drill inside the heads of that squadron of the damned, then the blast. Hardly believable, I know, because light travels faster than sound. And yet, and yet. I tried to tell them about Kovac's mute cries, tried to paint the picture of him cowering in the rubble, and completely blind: first his hands went to his neck, like he couldn't breathe, his legs gave way, he tore off his hazmat suit, including his rat-tail belt, and once all of that was off, his hands, in their fingerless gloves, went to his face. One important detail, dear tribunal members: when I say they went to his face, I mean he started rubbing or even yanking at his face, with such force he seemed sure to take out his own eyes. Not important, in fact, said one of the tribunal members, some big shot: their kind always have an aversion to the light. Another of the members, a bootlegger in former, calmer days, quickly asked how it was that I could be so sure about the reaction of Ź-Brigadier#317, also known as the Albýno, given that I had already stated—a sworn statement, if I didn't mind him pointing out—that the explosion had robbed me of my sense of hearing. But that's exactly why, I said: his mouth opened and closed, and although (because) there wasn't any sound for me at that point, the bulging tendons in his neck, close to bursting, made it clear how loudly he was screaming. Mr. Tribunal Member shifted uncomfortably in his seat. And the fact I remember his reaction at all, gentlemen, suggests just how violent it was, given I couldn't hear anything at that point. And I could still definitely see, unlike Comrade Kovac, whose light-averse retinas had already been fried. I saw other things too, I said. Like what? asked another of the men before me, a former pharmacist, fat and silver haired like the rest, though in his case he'd applied rather too much hair gel, very youthful. Like for example Comrade Morgan, I said, protecting his head and narrowly avoiding a falling joist. Like for example Comrade Serrano, I said, not narrowly avoiding a huge chunk of concrete, being pulverized. You watched him die, then, Brigadier#496? For example. It took a little while, I add. And we can see from the medical report that you yourself came away largely unscathed, a few bumps and bruises; what would you put that down to? Luck, sir, though I still don't know whether good or bad. Less of the riddles, 496: speak plainly. Oh, plain as the nose on my face, sir, clear as you like, and after that, dark, dark, dark. I could see, then I could see fuck all, then, a little while later, they came and pulled us out. And the buzzing noise? said another (storekeeper). Still there, sir. On and off, if you know what I mean. How long was it before you regained consciousness, 496? Couldn't say exactly, sir, but the rescue guys say they think I was out for twenty-four hours, possibly forty-eight. And was that when the hallucinations began, 496? Could be, sir, could be. And those comrades of yours who set the explosives, acting, we believe, with no ill intention: would you describe your attitude toward them as one of resentment? No, sir. Does anything lead you to believe that they could have acted out of malice, or that they may in fact have known the whereabouts of your unit? Nothing at all, sir. The explosives guys were just following orders, sir, doing their duty. (Their orders, their duty, their overweening fear, their empty stomachs, their months without proper sleep, their innate incompetence—AKA the principal defining characteristic of my compatriots.) Further clearing of throats, hushed voices. Then the head honcho, toupee, bushy mustache, raised his wooden, ruby-incrusted hammer and brought it down: Time to come clean, 496! he cries. What, exactly, is your relationship with the Noble Empire of Jakarta?

78.

The rats scurried over us and between. Can you hear what they're saying? asked Kovac. But everyone just ignored him. Nobody wanted to listen to old Albýno Kovac. We had quite enough to deal with, heads stuffed with the competing smells of shit, blood, and rotting meat. It was dawning on us, as we lay there in the rubble, that the rats weren't the problem. We couldn't see them, but we felt the weight of them through the suits. Big fuckers. Succulent, you might almost say; the stench around us had done nothing to stop our hunger. The ground shook every now and then, shifting the rubble. We assumed from the continued explosions that we were being looked for, so they gave us a certain hope, but at the same time we knew that each explosion might only have meant we were being buried deeper and deeper. Kovac reckoned it shouldn't take them more than a couple of days to get us out, because of how close to the treatment plant we were. How did he know how close to the treatment plant we were? The rats. It was the rats, too, who told him when Serrano expired. Kovac, as if in payment for the information, let the rats have free run of Serrano. He ordered me to get the suit off. Yes, I mean it, he said. What does he care now? Am I wrong, Serrano? At least that way the little fuckers will give us a rest, at least for a while. Serrano took his time dying. More than once we thought he'd taken his leave, not a peep for hours, days possibly, then suddenly he'd pipe up again, a low, broken whimper reminding us he was still there, that his half-crushed brain was still clinging on. You, he'd croak, you Atlantika fuckers, I tell you *I need a drink*. Followed by a very weird noise, cracked in more ways than one— made me think of a bird of prey calling out, having strayed into some unfamiliar territory. I'd reach my sleeve over to him and squeeze out a few drops of the mixed urines and oxides that the pipes above had been dumping on us from time to time. After one of these, Serrano stopped talking for good. Hard to admit, but what a relief for all concerned. Morgan was trapped beneath a joist, only the top half of his body was free. He clicked his tongue to let us know he was still alive, till one day he blurted out something else instead: Asunción. And I, muscle twitch–like, came back with: Paraguay. Castries, he said, and someone else, a voice from somewhere in the darkness: Saint Lucia! Stanley, I cried, and the walls sent back a ghostly, Falklands. Honiara: Solomon Islands. Tarawa: Republic of Kiribati. Siukville, said a voice from somewhere in the depths. And again: Siukville. To no answer. Where the hell is Siukville, I wailed eventually, and, since it wasn't possible for Morgan to laugh with that amount of cement and earth constricting his body, he gave a tired few tongue clicks instead. *Click, click, click*. I did manage a laugh, though the echoing cavernous spaces around us turned the laugh to something pained, a lament. I couldn't have cared less and went on making the same sound, same lament, louder and louder, more as a way to override the buzzing noise than wanting to fill in gaps in our geopolitical knowledge, because suddenly it was as though the ancient nun had appeared among us, calling us by the names she never learned, could never be bothered to learn, calling out from the depths of some body of water, very deep, very still, that rose occasionally—only very occasionally—so that we were nearly engulfed.

79.

It's close to midday. Birds, waves. Clara can't stand the light, snarls at me to shut the blinds. She still has the ragged bra in her hands. Again with the fabric, the elastics. And the *click, click, click.* In Clara's mind, extreme hunger is the way of the ascetic, a path leading to a certain kind of order. As though the density of you, and the grime, have to be gotten rid of before you can disappear. Before the stone crashes into the earth, cracking open its molten core: before I can get up and go out, thrusting open the door. But lo, Clara, the way she's breathing, her dull, untidy plaits, all tell me she's mislaid something she doesn't believe in: she's lost nothing, a portion of nothing, a unit of nothing, like the grimy nothing-coins scattered across the room, the nothing-dogs and their nothing-barking, like nothing-China and the nothing-vases it produces. I watch her going on, in silence. Then something comes into my body. The echo of something breaking, or barking, though bearing in mind the stone, it's sure to be nothing. I've got to go. I don't run, I push the door carefully the rest of the way, just about avoiding making any noise. Shut it behind me. She doesn't even ask where I'm going, because she's sure I'll be back. And the sound of the door clicking shut could be the sound of anything. But the stone takes the sound into it. It swallows it up.

80.

Nobody wanted to hear what Kovac had to say. Not even the rats. Kovac didn't care: emotional diarrhea had kicked in. His only seeming

concern was to make sure he lodged his final imaginings with someone, that someone being us. In the end it was he who took me back to
the hillsides of Manaslu, speaking in hallucinogenic Sherpa tongues,
apparently spurred into expression by the approach of death. I had
been there before. Familiar to me, the temperate coastal places, the
intricate metalwork, the palisades wrought from jade. All the while
Kovac, my guide, gave me an encyclopedic rundown of more or less
everything that had happened to him in childhood, the gross gen-
erosity of detail of a dead man: getting hooked earlier than most
on Vakapý; son of a miner's son; his first love; first heartbreak; the
'29 campaign; the year Ñandú III was crowned champion; seeing
that his destiny truly was on the Vakapý court; Ñandú III's "Sugar
Ahaka" year, dubbed by the sports journalists of the day as owner
of "the sweetest swing imaginable"; all the skirts he chased at that
time, all the epic nights out; tabloid attention; Ñandú III's sponsor-
ship by a famous brand of matches with a dandy-looking indigene
on the box; the matchboxes a collector's item, moms, dads, Albýnos,
and natives alike collecting them, everyone but everyone wanting a
piece of Ñandú III; and later, in the same narrative loop he kept up
for untold hours, slipping back and forth between digressions and
facts and minor facts, his great yarn, he described his fabled debut in
the Anguja: the frescos that used to adorn the Hall in those days, the
Ovid-like scenes on the murals, the revolving bar, the queues for the
betting counters, the winners demanding their money the instant it
was won, the rusted locker-room doors, the open gangster involvement in the outcomes of matches, the just as open racism and dis-
crimination, and finally a description of the season finale, which was
decided by the swing of a lesser player's ahaka, a dark (in fact pigmentless) horse of Atlantikan Vakapý. There were gaps in his story,
small chinks between which you could catch a glimpse of the high
plains and plateaus, the small lake surrounded by smooth boulders,
the covering of snow, the steepness of the slopes beyond, and the
peak itself, high up in the clouds, impossible to make out with the
naked eye.

81.

"As before: an exterminator does not eliminate rats upon catching them. When the trapped rats screech, it attracts more rats. You have to be patient, stay very calm. The whole world could collapse but you just wait. Hear them screeching? Not yet, stay put. Wait for more to gather, *then* go for it. That's what Morgan showed me."

82.

When I came to, Kovac was burbling—something about a labyrinth. I don't know how he managed to get us to that place, or how long the journey took. The form formerly known as Serrano was by now about half the size. We had not died yet, of which I'm sure because Kovac's story was so deathly boring: on and on it went, ungainly, full of pointless detail, of repetitions and half repetitions and sloping accumulations, so that the audience of rubble and rats and us, to all intents and purposes moribund—frangible, riddled with sickness, fodder for something—after seven days trekking through the snow had sunk down into a liturgy-like rhythm, a march, going on and on, but at the same time around and around, around in ever-so-slightly-deviating circles, veering out and in imperceptibly, crossing back and forth haphazardly over other contiguous circles, raveling, no stimulus other than the difficulty of making our way around or over or through that boundless geometry. As the possible paths multiplied, so the space inside our prison grew ever more constricted. Likely, very likely, we had all by now been infected. Kovac, yammering on. Gulping up our oxygen in one final diversion. We couldn't bring ourselves to shut him up, but nor were we ready to take his place. He'd go on until he ran dry, or until his words had made shriveled husks of us. Even the dead ends he ventured down, as well as the rambling digressions that went so wildly astray that they lost all contact with whatever he had been saying immediately before,

even these he found some way to prolong, skirting around any subject or notion of logical order that might allow us to orient ourselves.
I now believe that Kovac, fever-mad and short on oxygen, had perhaps taken it upon himself to provide a condensed version of all the
stories ever told, the nub, the rub, so that his own verbosity would
become an end in itself, irreducible, and truly 1:1 in scale.

83.

So then, continued Kovac, the king of the Albýnos had ordered the
construction of an underground labyrinth. A stone with which to kill
several birds: creating a barrier with the aggressive southern tribes,
for example, but also a legacy, something for people to remember him
by. It was by no means a spur-of-the-moment idea: he also envisaged
it as the most technically advanced creation in Albýno history, and
the completion of such a monument a cause for celebration among
his people and the envy of all outsiders. It was to be an impregnable
labyrinth. Though the king was known for his calm and levelheaded
nature, a part of him was conscious of the risk in such an undertaking. Nonetheless he decided to proceed. His name would go down
in the annals as a leader of great accomplishments, a philanthro-
pist king; not only would there be a place for him in the pantheon
of Albýno nobility but also among that of all great latter-day mon-
archs. The Royal Hydraulics Committee immediately set to work,
inviting tenders from the best architects. In the teahouses and skin
bars of the country, the talk was of little else. The man who succeeded
in building the perfect labyrinth would be rewarded with all the
gold from the largest mine in the land. Within weeks the first pro-
posal was presented at the palace, and others soon followed, differing
wildly in quality and hailing from the least expected corners of the
known world. They came accompanied with offerings for the king—
jewels, extravagant cloths, spices—but the designs themselves, to a
one, were of the utmost simplicity: gardens of winding paths, cheap

trompe l'oeils, traps and tricks to please a child. Nothing the king was satisfied with. As time passed he even began to feel that each jewel and incense-decked chest took him away from the reality of the construction he had first seen in his mind's eye. Soon—and in disproportion to the ever-decreasing number of offerings and tenders that arrived—rumors about the fragility of his mental health began to spread. Feeling himself far from the world already, he quit the court and went into a kind of exile, taking up residence in the tallest tower in the palace. In his solitude he came to think that the architects' inability to create the perfect labyrinth was in fact down to the question he had asked, or the way he had formulated it: he had posed it as a problem of spatiality and not of language. Maps, paths, layouts: none of the architects had been able to resolve the fundamental question of the labyrinth; they had each been seeking a *spatial* resolution to a problem of a different order altogether. They were overly concerned with beginnings and ends. A way in, a way out. Was that all it was? Would he allow his great life's work to be reduced to such generalities? Months alone in the tower led him to conclude that each of the sketches before him was but a replication of each architect's logical mind: these labyrinths had all been resolved in advance, and this was precisely how they had come to exist, at least on these sheets of paper. This is a labyrinth, said one of his ministers (said Kovac) the day they decided to break down the door to the tower to be confronted with a cadaverous, unkempt individual, his nails and beard long: he had renounced his rule until such a time as he found a solution to the torture he himself had instigated. Reams and reams of parchment lay around him, miles of it, and in the gloom—and in spite of the ministers' excellent Albýno eyesight—they looked like nothing so much as great piles of ermine rugs. In reality the hide scrolls were covered in the most intricate of script: thousands, millions of dashes and marks in red and blue, the red column on the left, the blue on the right. What is a labyrinth? asked the king. A labyrinth, Your Majesty, said one minister, is a place composed of paths that twist, fork, and overlap in such a way as to mislead any person entering therein. But the way out, said the king, is not something one should be concerned with: perhaps only the labyrinth itself ought to concern itself with questions of ways out. But, Majesty, with no way out and no promise of ever finding that way out, one would have a prison and not a labyrinth. These explanations, cried the king, who is it that speaks them? What is their relationship with the labyrinth—what order of importance do they possess *in relation to* the labyrinth? Are *you* a labyrinth? No, Your Majesty. Blaggard, you do not know that for certain. Truly: the perfect labyrinth has self-awareness, or comes to develop it. It adopts its guests, and these in time become the labyrinth itself, while at the same time new labyrinths take shape inside them, do you see? That thing you call a way out is but one more junction among so many others. It has nothing to do with the space separating *in* and *out,* which these upstarts seek to complicate in a purely linear way, but rather with the nature of the movement of things in that space, and what is lost—or found—there. Let us consider that the purpose of these entities, disoriented, trying to find their way, may derive not from what they do inside the labyrinth, but the other way round: their purpose determines which, out of all the experiences, will comprise the labyrinth. And it was then that the king understood that the ministers were bound forever to disappoint him, because to them any notion of space had first to pass through the filter of scientific knowledge; to them a labyrinth was a projection of specific volumes and mass, of *somewheres:* abstraction and rational process, over and above a field in which various bodies interact. A labyrinth, he concluded, is nothing but a way of seeing, just as seeing is a way of being in the world. And he also knew then that no architect would ever be able to do what he needed, and, with the help of the ministers, he got to his feet, giving the order for his court painter to be summoned.

84.

"The dogs are born deaf and with no teeth or claws."

85.

Señora Albýno#2460 barely looks up when I come into the stationery shop. Her long hair is in a plait: not my work, I'm sure. How long since my last time? The street outside is surprisingly empty, as though the gamblers normally lining it, as well as the usual sacks of cement and the trash cans, have fled the city. Been a while, she says, *been awhile,* before going back to what she was doing, which is filling little transparent plastic baggies with sequins, fifty or sixty perhaps in each, separating them by size and color. Any stations free? I ask, and she shrugs and starts to say something, but her voice is immediately drowned out by what sounds like a dogfight outside, the barking and braying too dementedly loud for anything else to be heard. Señora Albýno#2460 takes sequins from a larger baggy, and the smaller baggies she tears from a large roll with perforated joins; the roll, judging by its thickness and the dust covering it, looks just about infinite. At intervals she tears off a new baggy, which says "Made in China," to place on the counter, which looks like it takes some effort (the bulging vein at her temple). And she begins again, plunging her hand into the sequins, sorting them, making a scrapheap of defective ones to one side. Any stations going? I say. Been a while, she replies, in that low, unmistakably Señora Albýno#2460 voice. *Been a while.* And back to her task. Her forefinger moves reasonably quickly, not really very quickly if you bear in mind that in fact this is part of her job, something she does for a living, separating sequins—*one, two, three*—she isn't in a hurry, though sometimes the sequins are stuck together and she has no choice then but to employ her thumb and sometimes even her ring finger in prying them apart. Now, each of these stops and pauses, in themselves quite brief, and unto themselves not very significant, when you add them all up, plus add them to the manifold interruptions and distractions throughout the course of the day, interruptions and distractions, such as my arrival, finally result in a not-inconsiderable amount of dead time: an hour each day is seven hours a week, and given that time is nothing if not money, that's a not-inconsiderable amount of money. Once ten more baggies have been filled, five or six hundred shiny sequins in their rightful places, ready to go out on the shelves, Señora Albýno#2460 gives a flick of the head, and through I go to the back.

86.

In moments, the ragged breathing of the huddled forms synchronizes, falling into something like the rhythmic *putt-putt* of an outboard motor. I have to pick my way through them for a while before I come to a free station; I get in position, find a vein, and slide the needle in. Flash of goose bumps across my body, the opening jingle. The tedious tutorial for first-time gamblers, followed by the health warnings from the Department of Hygiene, followed by offers of free Credits in exchange for your vote: withal, the immeasurable sensation of freedom and comfort that comes when you plug in. You see the stats rattling away in the bottom part of the screen, you hear the echoing footfall of the plaýers crossing the courts. Here we are in the Vakapý realm, the cells and windows, the stadia and ball trajectories, which together contain both of us, the gamblers, and the twelve simultaneous matches, all part of the same continuously shifting stake, and in among it and variegating it and comprising it, the constant callouts and adjustments made by various bookmaker hubs as they try to configure the head-to-heads, the ever-changing odds, the translations for the gamblers tuning in from abroad, and the camera angles necessary for us to see the ahakas swinging and slicing the air. The ball comes back off the sloped tambul, and Aña IV dives to catch it millimeters before the second bounce, flying through the air, arm pistons fully extended, before crashing to earth. His opponent, a youngster just graduated from the Atahuâ youth system, runs up to the ref screaming, claiming traveling. The ref, barely looking at the irate plaýer, gives a weary shake of the head, as though this plaýer is well known for such theatrics, or all the plaýers are. The ref doesn't seem to be considering a video replay: that's what the rules are for. The player, who has turned a little purple from screaming, unstraps his aħaka and goes on imploring the ref, gesticulating wildly. The ref has turned away, motions for the game to go on. Above that game, on Window#7, Yagwatý X, rookie of the year two seasons ago, has just been trashed by Mýlpalta Man, who, though he appears to have put on a few pounds, is looking pretty untouchable: his heat map shows laser-precision shots from all over the court. In the bottom window, a doubles match on Intra-Klay—a synthetic clay sprinkled with water to make the going very slippery, and very high-speed—is being played at such a chaotic pace the two sides remain almost constantly neck and neck; neither can establish a clear lead. It resembles a pell-mell system of whirring pulleys and pistons, or a philharmonic ensemble on fast-forward. This is where I am, my mind, my very being spread across the different matches, tracking the twelve balls in flight, tracking the multitude of betting positions, and my dots soon start to appear without me thinking, with no conscious decision on my part: at first faintly, like the beginning of a rash, and after that increasing, seemingly splashing onto the screen, until I start to be able to synchronize them with the scores, and the columns begin to fill out like two processions of ants: reds marching down the left-hand side, blues down the right. Reds and blues: the dots, the premonitions of dots, flock behind the changing numbers, instantaneous and 100 percent accurate. Looks like I'm on a roll. Each time a player collects a ball in his aħaka and slings it at the wall, I'm up points. A blinding pink light begins to illuminate my station, spotlighting my face in the general gloom of the backroom, but who cares: I'm rolling. At first my gains are slight; I don't feel bold enough to come piling in with any big bets. But that starts to change. Who cares, I think. Really, who gives a shit. It's so seductive when you get on a roll, though in a sense it's just a more subtle way of deferring loss. But I'm not thinking about this. I'm winning, and I think about winning. About the winning feeling. About the faces of the others in the room, the losing faces, tiny, unrecognizable faces, now that I'm winning; how this joyfulness separates me from them, making all ugliness and suffering seem strange and far away. I see the Credits, the pixels splashed across my screen that signify Credits, all of those digits bumping one another up, up, up: they *are* Credits. Up I go, up to my eyelids in precious Credits. I ascend, though it is not an ascent you feel as such. Up, until I myself *become* Credits. And yet, alongside this ebullience, a still, small part of me vacillates: there is the very real risk that my streak will come to an end just as suddenly and inexplicably as it seemed to begin. When your luck's in, it's contingent, temporary, so delicate—or worse, maybe it isn't even me this is happening to . . . In among the images that course through my bloodstream courtesy of the needle, a shadow appears, one I recognize as belonging to the owner, Señora Albýno#2460, a faint smudge that is her, and a stab of nostalgia hits me, nostalgia for her comic strips, for those small shiny disks of hers in their sachets and their piles, for the hairdos I will no longer style for her once the world devolves into its natural end-state as one great carpet of molten lava . . . I see her signal to me to close my eyes, she's going to do an emergency disconñect. I nod, and the needle comes out with a little spray of blood—eyes still closed, I feel the warm spatter down my forearm. By the time I am able to blink again, a cluster of gamblers has gathered around me, and Señora Albýno#2460 is smiling. Felicidades, she says, *felicidades.* And they begin clapping—slowly, a smattering at first, before it becomes a full-blown round of applause. They start chanting, *And so say all of us, and so say all of us,* and lean in to embrace me. Smell of old sweat and meringues. Then we're all hugging, all of us together, an indeterminate amount of time like this, slathering one another in the mutual affection that, unbeknownst to us, has germinated due to all the time spent in this consummate togetherness: conñected to the one Vakapý source. Soon Señora Albýno#2460 tells everyone to calm down. Then, not without a large dose of shame in her voice, a voice edged with a metallic hum (like Grandma's), she says I need to make myself scarce. Get out of here, she says. *Get out of here.* They'll be coming for you, says one of the gamblers, a hairpiece guy. The Department. They'll assume you've gamed the Sýstem somehow. You should get going. As I gather myself and make to leave, Señora Albýno#2460 presses an enormous roll of paper into my hands. Take it up to Cordillera Hill, she says. You can cash it in there. We don't keep enough on the premises. There's an address, she says, under the serial number, your winnings and the number of points you got: it's a map. *It's a map.* This wasn't supposed to happen, right? Nobody planned for this. I make my way toward the exit, people's hands reaching out to touch me; everyone wants to touch me. Adiós, amigos, I murmur, half to myself. *Adiós, amigos,* with a wave of the hand. No one says anything in response. I'm at the door. I come through the stationery shop, which feels very empty without her in it. Without her in it, even the sequins look dull.

87.

Morgan was forever making things up. About doppelgängers, about visions. About people who appeared to be people but were in reality extraterrestrial outriders, advance parties from other worlds. These beings, he said, are the only reason the city is still on its feet. It was they who originally decreed that Atlantika should be erected here, and that our people should inhabit it. Do you really think the natives put up those marble temples single handedly? That they came up with those inverted-sun motifs without any influence from an alternate, extrinsic vision of our planet? Because in that time, before everything—the time before time, even—there was no such thing as engineering, not in the current sense, or not, at least, on planet earth, then barely more than a dark, glimmering rock, devoid of day and night, devoid of oceans, seas, seabeds of any kind, devoid of tektonik plates or any faults between them, devoid of vegetation, no fungal kingdom to speak of, parasitical pandemonium as yet unleashed, devoid of the great beasts that once walked the earth and the lesser creatures they dominated, devoid of the latter-day dominators, humankind, who went on to take everything for themselves only to fritter it away almost as soon as they held it in their hands: a dark, shining stone like the mirror of a river as yet incapable of irrigating any land, this was what Morgan said and also what it said in the notebooks he compiled out of newspaper clippings and other texts: that they had been around since then but were still among us, acting like us, passing themselves off as us though in fact they couldn't be more dissimilar from us, and that was why you had to be on your guard, and I nodded at all of this, not knowing if Morgan was being serious when he said that one day they were going to come for him and take him away to the Noble Empire, that he'd show me, I'd see, to which I replied, Sure, for want of anything else to say, just to carry on the conversation, really, when I simply couldn't bring myself to believe that those superior intelligences, minds from another galaxy, inventors of many marvels and highest technologies, could be perverse enough to deposit us on the exact point where two countervailing winds of such tearing strength collided like freight trains, and this I did say to Morgan, exactly this, and Morgan gripped his belly and laughed, baring those crooked teeth, groaning a little and laughing a little more before setting about setting me straight, setting that forked tongue of his in motion: he said it was beyond him how someone as fundamentally stupid as me had always come top in class and even got to be standard bearer on parade Mondays, truly incredible, because these minds, these intelligences, I was only so quick to deride them as such because there was no way to describe them, no image that could capture them: they weren't minds in the usual sense of the word, he only put it like that for want of something less apt, and it wasn't that *he* didn't have a better word, there wasn't one, and never would be. Thus spake Morgan.

88.

I take Avenida del Caudillo Insigne. There are people on the street. Far more than is normal at this time. Cordons, uniforms. Riot police, the mounted division. And the protestors. Chrysalids and Magnetized side by side, a great roiling mass, all together like one big family before the screens that have been erected by the Department of Communications and Fun in the main squares throughout the city. A scientist is being interviewed, a mob of microphones and flashing cameras around him: he says there's nothing to worry about, the meteorite isn't due to hit the earth for at least another sixty-five years. Ages. Yes, ages and ages. Hell, says an old woman beside me, who appears to have no teeth, that's enough time for another *two* Bugs to come and do their business. It ain't like it's gonna happen tomorrow. And I guess she's right. While all of this is going on, suddenly I see them. Two fat guys in suits, lounging oh-so-surreptitiously on the hood of a black Laputa GT—no plates—in dark glasses. They don't pretend not to see me; they're eating/drinking/slathering their faces in eggnog frappes and don't bother to hide the fact that it's me they've got under surveillance. My mind turns to the stone as I begin walking in the opposite direction, trying to blend in with the crowd. I think about Clara and look down at the coupon. If she was going to be proved right, it would have to be like this. Me being allowed to win.

89.

And I was joining things together. Joining what together? Words. Morgan wasn't. He was the boss, and all bosses concern themselves not with joins but with dissemination. He controlled the rumor mill at school with consummate care: control that, and you controlled the school. For him, words signified control. A careful throwaway remark in the ear of the right person was enough to keep everything going the way he wanted it to. I'm sure that it was Morgan who started the rumor about the novice killing herself because of a love affair. The (his) story went: the Mother Superior happened on the couple having sex in the confessional, a couple of hours after evening prayers. The novice was penanced severely, and the diocese was contacted to begin her excommunication. The identity of the Padre was never divulged, because that, they (Morgan) said, would have made the scandal even greater. Then one night while all the convent was asleep, the novice took a belt and looped it around one of the rafters. And that was that. In our school, seven o'clock mass was always held before the Monday evening parade. In our eyes all the different priests who gave sermons or offered us the wafers soaked in caterpillar juice were prime suspects as they stood before us. Following that first day back, when we came across the article about the novice on the reverse of a picture of a naked black woman with breasts like fear itself—endlessly ample—Morgan began constructing the story, reconstructing it thereafter with slight modifications each time, and sometimes it was Morgan who told it, sometimes others chimed in, added plotlines and characters, elements from unknown sources, poaching, appending, stealing, eventually creating a tale that bore little resemblance to the original, so that in the end what you had was a blended amalgam, itself a tranche of a larger collective fiction that at some point ceased to belong to us—if indeed it ever did—and took on a life and a trajectory of its own. From that precise moment on (though I couldn't say precisely when it was), I couldn't stop thinking about the novice either. No longer did I masturbate over Zulaýma or her planetary breasts, seemingly astral entities from some unknown solar system, but instead began hammering out my own version of the scene involving that young novice, gasping and sweating behind the latticed screen of the confessional. The Padre, one of their number or perhaps all of them at different moments, shoving her up against the rear wall, lifting her habit up with one hand, groping her exposed body with the other. A scene that repeated over and over, and over and over, always with Zulaýma superimposed in places, or parts of Zulaýma. It wasn't long before I gave up on the Page Threes altogether: it had to be dark, it had to be in my room, and it had to feature elements of that scene, otherwise zero hard-ons for me.

90.

This city has two great enemies: dogs and winds. Of the former there are far too many. The next pandemic is sure to come via the canine gene. Which animal shall we domesticate in order to exterminate the dog for us? We'll find a way, I fear. The wind, however, cannot be brought to heel: it gets inside your mind; it muddies and muddles and wreaks its marled havoc. One massive airflow comes down from the eastern Sierra, picking up all manner of sediment along its westerly way, before being confronted by an onshore wind the moment it hits Atlantika. Therein its potency. It dries out the land, it lays waste to the flora. It ties you in nervous knots before yanking your sanity out wholesale. In the later part of the day, only a light ambient buzzing—not much different from the gnawing of rats in the telephone wires. But then, once night descends, something closer to a static roar sets in: I imagine a slaughterhouse at dawn, in the moments before the meat is distributed, as the long line of pigs begins to thin and the hormones and the sweat and the smell of blood send the animals into strange attitudes, strange teeth grinding, heaving noises drawn from their snouts. Then plastic, then methodicalness. But not here; here the wind is all. The winters are the worst: people just don't go out. The life of our public spaces, and of the stones comprising them, depends on the summer pursuits of visiting tourists. Some years, the February cold extends well into spring, and though the sun begins to show its face, and though a little humidity enters the air once more, the wind in its raw and roaring state does not desist. It tells us what to do. It is a matter of some seriousness for the inhabitants of this city.

91.

I come out of the vision, or go back to it. One or the other. Clara sets herself, focuses. She is thinner than ever, thanks to the latest catastrophe in this our great city: it's springtime (just like now) and suddenly the coastal waters have stopped producing fish. Most years, the fisherfolk spend all day out on the water, from before dawn until dusk, before separating the catch at the docks and getting royally drunk down there too. But this isn't most years. A year of sickness. Still they get up in the dark, in spite of the anguish of their sleepless nights, in spite of the almost total absence of food on tables, the interminable protests organized by the Unions, who knows whether they are playing for time, or attempting to come to terms with the loss, or, less likely, trying to find some way out of this incident—this is the way people have been referring to it, the incident, as though wanting to avoid naming it, or wanting to name it only by omission, not coupling it with the concrete fact suggested by our shared history, an incident, they say, in order to give it a possibly irregular and ill-defined form, but a form all the same: the incident begins to take shape in the lee of the palm tree sheltering the protestors from the rain. Its artificiality and its consensual nature are one and the same, given that its form, its true shape, is silence—is it not? And it therefore is named on the basis of its extremities or outer lineaments, which themselves originate in what is not really known: in the afflicted looks of the five or six boatmen sitting in a circle on chairs rocked by the waves, in the circumlocutions that prove to be the outer edges of circumlocutions, in understanding one another perfectly, all understanding that, from a certain moment, everything they might discuss or omit will relate irremediably to the incident. When the ever-present bottle is nearly empty and all gossip and small talk of the day has been covered or has simply ceased to matter in the sudden cool of the encroaching darkness, when the sun has set on the implements of their trade, ridiculous rods and tackle in a time when there is nothing for rods and tackle to haul from the water, only then may the incident be addressed with the necessary care. Ignoring it outright would be nearly as vulgar as trying to give it a precise name. But still they try to do both. And the attempts are vulgar but give them a lift all the same. To avoid the sun ever catching them with feet on dry land is part of an overall and intuitive effort to save themselves; stubbornness and superstition are all they know. And yet the best they manage is a few horse mackerel—on a good day. Anything else brought up in the nets is worthless. Days go by, and the catches remain at record lows. The younger guys are the first to throw in the towel: the pull of the waters has yet to embed itself in them, and they sell off their boats and all their gear and either head up into the Sierra or take a bus to the capital to try their luck in one of the factories or in the kiosks. It's all over the papers: "Fish Prices Soar." They say there's none left. That finally the Atlantik has stopped producing. This is a place in which people live not only on what the sea provides but also in the manifold occupations that accompany the servicing of it, and panic quickly sets in. Looting, cars being burned, scenes reminiscent of the time the Department of Hygiene denied that the Ź-Bug had gotten out of control. At that point all and sundry, mothers, fathers, brothers, and any grannies they could press into service, came out onto the streets to abuse us, to smash shop fronts and bus stops while the news crews came out in almost equal force to film the placards and the pictures of the deceased and the pictures of those who had disappeared. Fucking plumber scum! they screamed, as glass and dung rained down. When it was us—nobody else!—who had gone and gathered up the bodies of their children! Obviously the Atlantik, for the people who take their name from it, is a delicate subject—just as delicate and mysterious as the Bug. Up there, maybe even, with Vakapý. The Fishing and Marine Resources Department refuses to take responsibility. It's unusual in the extreme for a public body to openly give in like this: far more usual for their kind simply to lie and say everything's fine, they can handle it, they are in fact handling it, despite appearances. And with no head, unsurprisingly enough, the body quickly begins to fall apart: in this case, a wholesale failure to regulate sailing times, chaos in the chartering of vessels, no security measures at the docks, and an abrupt end to the usual muster of sailors. Even the most corrupt of the union bosses start to worry that their private stockpiles won't see them through winter. One of the few fishermen who has stuck at it carries on getting up in the dark, rolls up his nets, cleans his hooks, checks and calibrates the rigging. He creeps out of the house, trying not to wake his wife, and rows away from the harbor. It is a day spent alone in the eye of a storm that only he can perceive. It is day after day spent in this way: casting his line, waiting. Wind- and wave-buffeted, each bearing down on him with his noticing—like rabbit punches in boxing, delivered repeatedly and in the end devastatingly to the back of the head, jeopardizing your spinal cord. Then one day he comes home to find his wife not there. On this particular day he's back in daylight: he has decided to return early in an attempt to confirm or rule out recent nagging suspicions. These days and weeks at sea—the only thing that has gotten him through them are his constant thoughts of different ways to kill her. There is no particular basis to his suspicions, rather a certain asymmetric congruence, the same conviction that has convinced him the only way to end this is restitution has led toward the tragic denouement. She isn't home: guilty. Unbeknownst to him, she's gone out for sugar. He takes a leisurely look around their little shack to check she isn't there—nope, nobody is—then decides to sit down and wait. What a bother it would have been to come up with another explanation. The wife returns shortly before nightfall to find him sitting on the armchair with the orange sailcloth upholstery. The moment she's within striking range he falls on her, a flash of the descaling knife. Later on, he dumps the body out at sea. Nobody comes around asking where she is. A number of weeks pass and a fisherman—not him— brings the tattered corpse up in his nets. Newspapers across the region cover the story, and it lingers even in those of the capital city for a couple of days. As the motives are picked over and blame apportioned, the two fishermen each go on the defensive: the one everyone assumes did it, the husband, and the one who had the shitty luck of discovering the body. Then the reporters go back to their respective cities and the world once more forgets about this self-important little town. But, strangest of all, the surfacing of the dead woman is followed by a return to the Atlantik's prodigious fish-producing ways: it immediately starts spitting enormous, unprecedented specimens into the nets. People don't even have to take boats out to secure the incredible catches: fish start to appear, unabetted, in the bays and inlets all along this stretch of the Atlantik. A story I forgot all about, until a day came (also in spring) when Clara and I were walking by the docks, and she pointed a man out. He wasn't the standout feature of the scene that presented itself to us: he was standing next to a rich boat owner, the real focal point in the midst of a large crowd. The boat owner, dripping in gold, had a couple of assistants with him, sent down by a sardine-fishing company in the North, and was wearing a pair of bottle-green glasses, a woolly hat with a golden trim, and a magnetic bracelet on his wrist. Also, around his neck, a cravat made of semitransparent silk with an exotic pattern: a pair of dogs eating each other's tails. He was standing on a small dais fashioned out of crates, and the tips of his deck shoes, polished to a high gleam, rested on the prow of a small boat while the crowd pretended to hang on his every word. Speech over, the non-standout man handed him a bottle of sparkling wine that the boat owner then smashed against the side of the boat. The crowd clapped. What a joke; I wanted to die of embarrassment, vanish, for the waters to rise and swallow me. But Clara told me to look again, not at the sailor but at the man who had passed him the bottle. There was nothing to distinguish him: a supporting actor in every sense. Came out of prison a few months ago, Clara said. The jury blamed it on the wind. The Atlantik-Farers Union soon appointed him Spokesperson, then Deputy Representative. If he plays his cards right, he's gonna have a nomination for Rep to the Fishing and Marine Resources Department, right at the top. So it goes, I said. Clara stood looking out across the water.

92.

Morgan deserted a few days after being given the all clear by the medics. He'd been talking about setting out again, resuming the journey. The twinkle in his eye was a giveaway, that gelatinous, distant gleam, like the fish you see at market laid out on the ice in hottest August: I knew he was on his way. He was like that for several days and then disappeared, didn't even bother to make it official with a letter. His disappearing acts were pretty common by then. He'd go, he'd come back, little explanation. We were on body-gathering duties again. The Ź-Bug was into its final stages, but the bodies were just as dead as the first ones had been. He made his getaway while we were carrying out a routine operation on Cordillera Hill, which had by now been converted into the Zone CH trash-processing area in the Heroes of '58 Housing Project. To be honest, Cordillera Hill had always been a dump anyway. We found his hazmat suit in a skip on our way back from the inspection site. Nobody was overly worried, not even me. I pictured him, still in the undersuit, running off between the scattered needles, latex gloves tied at the thumbs, ash-covered urinals. Later on it occurred to me that in this reckless dash, surgical mask still covering his mouth, the big work boots on his feet and antireflective tape strapped all over his body, Morgan would have resembled one of those extraterrestrials whose movements and motivations he claimed such intimate knowledge of. We used to get bussed from HQ to an inspection site and back, and that day the return journey was interrupted by me standing in the middle of the road. The driver honked his horn. You don't want to spend the night in a place like this, he called down to me. We're missing a guy, I said; we can't go without him. But he didn't know who Morgan was, he'd never heard of him. At HQ that night, our unit captain read out his name a couple of times, just twice, before crossing it out. A couple of lines in ink was enough to bury him: Morgan ceased to exist. Three days after his disappearance his locker was assigned to a new recruit, a talkative type. He wanted to know everything there was to know about the tunnels. About the explosion, the nights down below, the Bug. His head was full of stories. Kovac, who had only partially recovered his sight, acted as though he was also deaf. The new boy had heard that only one of us survived the explosion—half survived—and he was dying to shake him by the hand. People said, he said, that the brigadiers had eventually been forced to eat one another, and that the last survivor had started in on his own body before he was pulled out—had started with his right arm. He wanted, had to, was dying to know more. I felt like telling him not to worry, that the worst was past. That the Ź-Bug was on its last leg, that people died in the tunnels, yes, but they were dying above ground too. But something prevented me. Killing rats, I said to the new boy, taking them out in the tunnels and in the grain stores and in the slaughter-houses, is a respectable job, respectable as any job you'll find, and not just that: it's a way of being somebody in the world, kiddo. I told him about Morgan—the guy who'd survived—and about his vision of the exterminator's office as one of the fine arts, about the day he broke the rat-collecting record, about how as a kid he'd go and steal mini pinwheels and bangers from the Chinese stalls at market, about Zermeño, Birdface Helguera, Fatty Muñoz, the Page Three stash, about the time el Chino Okawa was stupid enough to say something about Birdface's mother and Morgan had to drag him the length of the schoolyard on his face until his face was like meatballs, and not because Morgan was upset about the insult, far from it, but because in order to rule, you have to set down the rules, boundaries that no bastard may transgress, boundaries that are there *even if you can't see them,* even if it's all smiles and pats on the back, and that by the mere fact of their existence, by giving the appearance of a beginning and an end, and of an amniotic zone, why don't we call it that, in between, become elemental, elemental in the sense that if any bastard should infringe them at all, even just a mini, minute, miniscule infringe-ment, then a punishment has to come down, regardless of whether said transgressive bastard knew of said elemental boundary rule, or was just, whatever, preoccupied. Kovac squinted up at me, eyelashes like alabaster pins. He wanted to talk as well. To tell the new guy about the noises, all the advances he'd been making in his theory of furtive rat language. But the new boy was mine now, mine, all mine. Kovac was going to have to find some other sucker to lead into his mountains. Some other fool who wanted to go back. You can always find one or two of them, oh, just busting to go back. All stories are, to some extent, a return. That night, before going into the mess for dinner, I was suddenly aware of the pressure of my tongue pushing against my teeth, poking them, nudging them contrariwise to the gums. The gums themselves had a rubbery consistency, rubberlike elasticity. The space between each of my teeth grew wider and my tongue was identical to that of a lizard: forked halfway along. I spied the new boy ahead of me, just going into the mess hall. Catching up with him, I placed a hand on his shoulder. Hey, kid, I said, just one thing: *patience.* That's what you need in this job, patience. It's no good going rushing in the second you hear the first little squeak, screech, or scratch. No, no. If you can learn to wait, you'll go far: any sap knows how to blow a tunnel to smithereens, not all of them have got what it takes to wait for the right moment. Could be that you've got talent, kid. This job isn't for jokers, right? The people need us. It's us keeping this city on its feet. Can you imagine where they'd be without us? Propping up a pile of rotting corpses, that's where. Pure and simple. *Listen* to the rats. Sing to them—and hear how they sing back. Who's to say they won't be naming streets after you one day?

93.

"Dogs have color vision, but they don't perceive all the same colors as us. They go around in relative darkness. Also that means they can see ghosts. And earthquakes."

94.

The following summer, after the Ź-Bug's definitive defeat was announced, tourism returned to Atlantika. The strain had been stabilized, and a vaccine rolled out. It must have been the wind. Rats are susceptible to the wind as well. It was the wind that finished them off, must have been. We were in the papers, and on TV too—"Pied Pipers of Hamlýtika," they called us. But we didn't do shit: it was the wind. Nonetheless some praise was heaped; you could blame the wind for things, not really place a garland around its neck. Once the quarantine was lifted and people started returning to their homes and their normal lives, the normal vicissitudes of life came back too, all the little issues, good health and time allowing, that you can plague yourself with. Street cleaners stopped bringing in dead children, the cemetery became a place of peace once more, and we were forgotten about. Since the day I took off my hazmat suit, I haven't seen a single rat in the streets.

95.

I have an idea: break the stone up into smaller fragments and use each of the fragments as noise traps. An idea, I ought to point out, that I haven't plucked out of the air, but that's based on the same mathematics that govern the trajectories of the Vakapý ball, and indeed the probabilities spawned by each and every shot. If we run the correct tests, look at the air currents, maybe do a few scale models, I'm convinced that we can come up with the precise configuration of these traps. Particularly at the times when humidity levels become unbearable, we'd be able to reduce the effect of the torrents of air that are a tyranny in our streets. You'd still be able to feel the warm blocks of air rushing about, crashing into one another, but the attendant noise would be negligible. In the lee of each fragment, placed strategically where the winds come in most strongly, you would have sanctums of quiet reaching as high as the tops of the palm trees: a protective belt some fifteen by three hundred meters. The suicide rate would drop, without question. And for my scientific brilliance, the keys to the city: mine. Thereafter, the birth of me as political animal, the emergence of my public-spirited, popular-servant self, bursting forth in a way everyone wishes it could burst forth in or from themselves: this, in reality, being our favorite part of ourselves. No two ways around it: our greatest vice lies in our need to serve. The party elects me leader. My first official act, probably, erecting a statue in honor of the exterminators. A monument to those fallen doing their civic duty—this is in gold lettering at the foot of the great man, his belt studded with many dead rats. Yes. I hit the hustings, reeling out the same catchphrase time after time, until, before my penultimate speech, a shrewd consultant, some genius of the campaign trail, tells me to drop the thing about my time in the Ż-Brigade. Comrade, he says, the people don't like slaughter and death, all of that. Then, following the customary vote rigging, there's a hiccup in the ordering of the multimember districts and I bomb out of the race, or I let myself bomb out, because the party then has the chance to come to my rescue, giving the guy who won my seat a department to oversee, not a big department but one that comes with a number of perks, including an office with two windows of its own and ten days' paid vacation a year. Several terms later, following a respectable, nay, distinguished tenure, I get a boulevard with my name on it. Oh, an artery rather discreet in length and moderate in flow of traffic and persons, broken at a couple of points by roundabouts, roundabouts, truth be told, put in those places out of sheer random caprice over and above any feeling or consideration for the geometrical requirements of the road network. So there is the need to come to terms with its humble dimensions, the slightness of the honor: four benches, two wheelchair ramps, a central reservation overrun by ferns. That is all—that is me. The blocks along which my boulevard runs, what is more, fall under a new regulation stipulating that each of the diverging streets must firstly be reinforced by fragments of the stone, and secondly must diverge at precise forty-five-degree angles from the principal thoroughfares of the Old Town. Just at the point where First Street begins, just south of that axis and positioned north south, a bronze plaque is the forerunner to the eventual bust that will take my place in the world once I have gone. Thus the efficient practices in this country—history, civic responsibility, and geography—all ticked in the same box: all prosperous citizens have the right to be reincarnated as a statue. As for Clara, who by now takes the form of stone fragments, or traps, if one prefers, she'll hang in pieces from every tree, a hundred little Clara-bells for the city, the smell of her will inundate my junctions and she will protect me from the ravages of airborne chlorine, oxygen, and brine. Again, it will all happen again, floods, droughts, freezes, hurricanes, earthquakes, plagues of locusts and rats: they will keep on coming, but not a single soul will stand up to accept the blame. Our fear is to be directed solely at these microscopic particles, microscopic but substantial all the same, caused by the disintegration of some consumable, possibly the clouds that come about in the grinding down, or otherwise disintegration of solid minerals carried on the wind. There that bust will stand, as proof of the efficiency of our systems, a head with time always to spare, no place to be, paused in midair in the middle of a boulevard where the wind does not, cannot blow. And it will be Clara, only Clara, who upholds the integrity of this area of calm, in the very place where the Bug first arose.

96.

Addendum to idea: when I ask for my boulevard to have its very own median and for this median to be fitted in turn with a row of banana trees, Dos Bocas banana trees, the Secretary for Hydraulic Resources and Social Wellbeing gives me a tender look and exclaims: Don't push your luck.

97.

In spite of the name, Zulaýma de Garay Boulevard is a pissy little alleyway lined with bright-red gravel. Every footstep raises a little clayey puff, until soon my gum boots are caked in it. The sky, in contrast, is wan and washed out: over the deserted huts on the shoreline, it could almost comprise a chunk of some kind of dissolvent. The huts lead haphazardly in the direction of the Heroes of '58 Housing Project, just about visible in the distance. The vision also affords shimmering snatches of ventilation units: though the homes are still too far away to be entirely visible, each seems to have an air-conditioning apparatus tacked on. Each is also possessed of its own peculiar sound, which depends on the materials that have been used in its construction, the number of people living in it and the kinds of things they get up to, and the camber of each plot. To one side of these homes, the inlet, and to the other, a bare hill of blackish, blasted soil and cinder paths leading between a slum of cardboard and corrugated-iron shacks. Of the temple that stood here fifteen hundred years in the past, where the natives sacrificed goats, virgins (not very often), and, of course, children, no trace. A couple of presidential terms ago, Housing and Welfare made the decision to turn the area nowadays known as Cordillera Hill into a project: twenty-eight identical subsidized tenement lodgings. The lucky ones, those who turned in their registrations in time, were then crammed in together with their families, distant relations included, friends and vague acquaintances included, in the single-person "transition huts" that were provided. Getting up to Cordillera Hill on foot is easier said than done, so I stand and wait for a bus to come. And stand and wait. And in the end decide to walk, worried above all about the goons from the Department of Chaos and Gaming catching me flat-footed, with the coupon from Señora Albýno#2460 on my person. As I advance, the project reveals itself in sections. In the far distance, at the center of the grid of gated sections, stands CH. It so happened that the inauguration of the project coincided with the abolition of *ch* as the fourth letter of the official alphabet, due to the fairly obvious fact that *ch* isn't one letter but two, and after that the Environment Agency had to get involved in order for the section with the now-defunct letter designating it to be used as a dump, in order to save the Housing Department from further ridicule while simultaneously falling in line with the new eco-policies that ever since then have been the nonnegotiable credo of a tiny but voluble portion of the city's populace. A third, perhaps center, position between the Magnetiźed and the Chrysalids, concerned about dwindling natural resources and forever putting forward innovative technologies to renew them. A metal sign with CH in large letters, presided over by an image of an angry toucan, tells me I've arrived. I cast my eye over the enclosing wall: slogans and candidate lists for upcoming elections run the length of its brickwork, which overlooks and provides a kind of corral for the great mound of burning trash inside. Around its edges stand dozens of houses fashioned from anything and everything that falls by the wayside of the dump. A number of years ago, a documentarian from the capital tried to sell a story, plainly false, about the people in CH providing themselves with food from the pickings at the dump. No, no, that doesn't happen: there's plenty for everyone to eat, there's the CH sandwich quota, don't you know. All kinds of plenty, sure, sure. Which means that, though they live in the very epicenter of the infection, they can't complain: they get free sandwiches, there's a permanent rent freeze, and their windows, though boarded up, over-look the lovely Atlantik itself.

98.

I am going to meet up with the boys. To look for them. The door to 395-B, section CH, Heroes of '58 Housing Project, is of strange con-struction: studded metal, with paint (once upon a time flag green, though now closer to squashed-olive gray) coming away in strips, and identical in size, design, and materials as 395-A and 395-C, which stand to either side—identical, also, to the doors to the rest of the tumbledown huts in CH. All molding and deteriorating under the caustic influence of the filthy air in the environs of the dump fires. The peephole, which is crooked and too low down to show any-thing but a portion of the visitor's stomach, must have some kind of mirror system rigged into it, some way of hiding the resident at the moment he or she comes to the door. A terrible moment for both parties, with the one behind the door given little option but to open it and confront the intruding presence, and the one outside having to stand and wait—has he just seen a shadow, something, moving inside? What could be behind the door? An animal of some kind? Or did he imagine it, and really no one's in? Maybe someone is, but she or he hasn't heard, is in the shower or enjoying her or his favorite Vakapý-related show on TV. After waiting for a while, shifting on his heels, trying not to think about the passing minutes, those passing minutes nonetheless add up and begin to weigh on him, weigh so much that something breaks—or is about to break, because there it is again: the shadow moving beyond the peephole. Someone breathing? An eye blinking but trying not to blink as the person inside is shocked to realize their eyelashes in motion may give her or him away? But the door is not answered. The form to which the shadow belongs does not step forward. I knock for a fifth time, five times more forcefully now, and though the door doesn't appear to have been fully closed, it does not budge. And that means I can't be completely sure that what the stone has shown me is accurate: that on the other side of this door there is a beautiful, immaculately finished room, wonderful polished-cedar surface and flooring—Kashmiri cedar. The coupon from Señora Albýno#2460: that's my ticket to get inside. Should anyone challenge my presence. Why am I here: here, this is why. I can *feel* them: on the other side of all of these doors, eyes, millions of eyes, like glimmering blue and red dots, looking out at me. A flicker of light appears at the edge of the door, as though a presage to the storm. A little wider. I step inside, slowly. And there it is before me, the valley: multicolored prayer flags in the distance, hoisted, fluttering like birds at play, between the tops of the poles and the stones in a line.

99.

The golden city, with its pavilions and watchtowers, what has become of it? All that remains is the snow, so red and uneven. I discern lines, marks. Foundations. Strange: my feet leave no tracks. The snow reforms each time I pick up a foot, draws back together as if nobody has been here. I must have gone the wrong way, I think. I've been away so long—I refused to come back for such a long time—that must be why. Or because I've come back blindly, feeling my way—I didn't actually know I was coming back at all.

-1.

The valley may be many miles long, but the storm has reduced the visibility such that each step becomes a leap of faith: though generally I keep my hands wrapped around me, hugging myself to conserve heat in the swirling icy flurries, I can barely see them if I do lift them in front of my face. As the incline steepens, the path narrows, worming its way up a defile with sleet water running down the banked snow on either side: coursing redly by, no rucks or crests at all, it gives the impression of lava stopped midflow. The glacier above, also brightest red, from which this water descends, is a vague looming shape through the blizzard; in less hostile weather, it serves as a beacon by which to orient oneself, but for now I must rely on the punched holes in the coupon, which I remove from my pocket at intervals; they are my only guide. Then again, a poor guide: the scaling of the tiny perforated coupon-map is either off or for some other reason impossible to transfer onto my physical surroundings. Onto *this* situation. I pat my coat where I normally keep my compass, but it's gone, and then, here, here, my provisions bag, my climbing rope, the ice axe, and the crampons—all gone. I pause, momentarily knocked off my stride, before continuing to climb. Soon I reach the crevice. It's very narrow: I drop onto my haunches and inch myself inside, barely. But it still seems worth stopping, waiting for the storm to pass, difficult as the wait may turn out to be, particularly because I am unsure how high up the valley I've come. The problem being that I'll freeze to death. I wait, I wait, and the cold begins to feel like splinters in my bones. I think of collagen hardening between carti- lages. I think of my icelike joints and bony tissue, stalactites inside me. I think of Clara and go on thinking about her, am still thinking about her when suddenly the ground begins to shake, a rumbling tremor, the bank of snow surrounding the crevice suddenly danger- ously alive. I try to tell it I haven't heard it. I try to trick it. But soon, an abrupt dimming of the already scanty light discernible through the opening. An eclipse, is my first thought. An eclipse. Fakir-like, I poke my head out and see it coming. Finally. An enormous wave painting the sky the color of blood.

-2.

I am assailed by an image of a man lying on the steps up to the four temple portals, while I, still crouching in the crevice and almost entirely covered in snow, try to keep myself from turning to ice. The man, on his back on the marble steps, arms outstretched, is wearing a hazmat suit, and his helmet visor is steamed up. I see the temple also from the perspective of the prone man: the half-open door he peers in through, the embossed golden serpent, the scales along the belly, large and skillfully rendered—rendered in such a way that they do not seem to register the change as they cross onto the next section of wall, where brick turns to marble, in spite of the alteration in mate- rial and the infinity of alterations in the soil beneath, the infinity of years, ruptures, movements, changes in weather: the serpent, the coil- ing, looping body of the serpent, retains an uncanny uniformity in its appearance all the way along. And now the man, with some effort, sits up, wheezing grimly: not the noise of the magma that contin- ues to stream beneath the temple foundations but that of his cold muscles creaking into motion once more, blood pounding as the invader-oxygen goads it into motion, tissues separating and rejoining, a cracking like that of dry sticks inside the suit, the gum boots, the gloves. When finally he manages to get to his feet, he stands staring at the four portals. No knocker on them, no bell to ring, and only darkness at their edges, and each guarded by a pair of enormous goddesses in dark stone, eight goddesses all representations of the same goddess, the upper halves of the bodies bare and the breasts disproportionately large. He picks one of the doors at random. He thinks he picks one, thinks his choice is random, and thinks that chance prompts him to think these things.

-3.

As the glacier continues to erupt around me, icy red floes rushing past, I continue to see the man and am reminded of the ash figures scattered across Upper Curumbý. The nuns took us on an excursion once to see the charred villages. Very educational, that outing, so fantastic: even if the figures in their death throes, and the smell of burned flesh, may somewhat have blurred the experience, those figures are part of our national heritage, monuments to the customs and habits of an era we know little about. You're not allowed to touch, but at the end of the guided tour, having made your way through the endless shanties and past the petrified forms of their erstwhile inhabitants, you're given the chance to buy broken-off fingers, fingers found among the remains that, with no blackened body attached, are made available for tourists to take home. The job of harvesting those souvenirs is endless too: a thumb or pinkie beneath every rock you care to pick up. In Upper Curumbý they make a life as stonecutters, and so it is with the man crouching in his niche. Stone-cold bones. Spasmic cadavers, and their natural transformation into works of art, are deeply rooted in Jakartinese culture, as evidenced by the murals that line the interminable passageway along which the other man now makes his way—having moments earlier crossed one of the thresholds, at random—while the frozen man continues to watch: perhaps by virtue of a predeath dream state, or as part of the connection that exists between death and dream. The man halts every now and then to take in another section of the mural, and having done so a few times—advanced, stopped, and admired—realizes that a single phrase is written repeatedly along the wall, threaded into the design. Though it's in a language he does not know, he can somehow read it: "And a woman came through the sands to the City." The faces of the figures, some of which drop away in plaster fragments, also repeat: surrounded by flames, surrounded by frost and snow, run through with spears, sliced away at neck and shoulder, martyrs of plagues and starvation: a moving tour of the natural history of the Noble Empire, exclaims a thundering voice, from inside his head, he at first thinks, from some unidentifiable but certainly finite inner space, somewhere between the first and last portion of the small intestine, to be precise, but that in reality issues from the unidentified bulk on a dais up ahead, a heap covered in a silk cloth, the cypress-wood dais at the end of the down-sloping passageway, past more and more engraved human heads and heads of dogs that hold up the pillars and try, twisting around, to bite his ankles as he passes.

-4.

The bulk or heap is neither a bulk nor a heap. I see now. I don't know what that makes it, and the man doesn't go over and remove the silk cloth, but it's also clear that its principle characteristics do not include those of heaps or bulks. What is more, in the moment he takes his eyes off it, it disappears, or rather, just as he starts to take in the detail of the cloth, the colorful, interwoven threads, the artfully hidden knots, semi-invisible as though embroidered long ago, as though embroidered at the beginning of time or maybe even before that and not by human hand, and the lifelikeness of the embroidered dogs that bend back around on themselves to bite their own tails, their teeth sharp and their tongues long and lolling, and the near-perfect surrounding circle that creates the sensation that the rest of the images are caught inside a swirling spiral, though the circle itself is interrupted by what we might call half-worlds or microworlds, starting in the empty borders and continuing, smaller to larger, until they reach a snarled tangle of carrion-eating flowers in the center, in that moment the bulk supposedly lying in a heap-like pile ceases to be there. And where before there had been a rather plain dead-end passageway, now a farther four paths appear. The man carefully considers his options. He takes a step, certain this is the way back to the steps, but coming through the door instead finds himself in a tiled patio, the tiles obscured in places by dun, brownish-gray grass spilling in at the corners and as high as his knees in places. He turns back, and the door has disappeared. He shakes his head: How can that be? The patio's four walls are the same color as the sky above, which means that as he looks up it is impossible to see where they end and it begins, though something tells him it will not be easy to scale them. Exhausted and as far as he can tell completely trapped, the man crumples to the floor. He starts undoing the suit. The air as it contacts his skin is warm, almost hot. He folds up the suit, places it to one side with boots and gloves, and soon falls asleep. A heavy, easy sleep, so deep and restful that the man, his being, begins to disentangle from his slumbering form. A sleep that exists in the margin of sleep. He is floating. Just a few centimeters off the patio floor at first, but then rising a little higher, and higher, a smooth and accelerating ascent, picking up pace. The sky above gray, but comfortingly gray. He feels no vertigo—the opposite, perhaps. At a certain height, the walls on either side drop away or give way to a transparent, glass-like substance as his sleep-being continues to ascend, so the city is revealed away and below, like a miniature model. And now suddenly the sky, the vaulted surface he thought of as the sky, drops away as well, to be replaced by a darkness, dense and inky black, opacity itself—though, now, sliced asunder by an enormous hand that reaches down toward him. Tremendous hand, tremendous fingers, every crease and wrinkle and fingerprint big as a road, and the dirt beneath the fingernails like enormous swampy expanses. Nor does the giant, of which the only thing he can glimpse is its forearm and hand reaching ponderously through the air, provoke any kind of anxiety in him. No, it's as though he knows the giant, feels what the giant feels, a quasi affection for the giantness of the giant, such that when it reaches down past him and begins to flatten the homes and buildings of the city, sweeping them aside and causing untold destruction and havoc, a strange feeling of peace blooms inside him, as though none of this has anything to do with him, or with the world.

-5.

When he wakes, the bulk or heap is him. Everything is as it was previously on the patio except for in one of the corners, where someone has installed an improvised dais and hung a length of velvet from a metal bar like a stage curtain. The velvet is threadbare, and the whole thing looks liable to topple at any moment. The man, an able carpenter, finds himself speculating—if speculating is the word when there's a good deal of fascination in the mix as well—engaged in enthused speculation as to the origin of such inexpertly worked woods. He begins counting rings, comparing the different grains, when a movement on the other side of the curtain catches his eye. His first instinct is to go over and investigate, though his eagerness itself gives him pause: he is suspicious of it. Eagerness of body, he was told long ago, should never go hand in hand with zeal of spirit. It is possible to separate the two, respond differently to one and the other. And yet, and yet, he does go over, he does look: putting his eye up to a gap in the curtain, he is presented with the sight of a group of nuns dancing around what appears to be a bulk, or a heap. No more than twenty of them, though they give the impression of being far more numerous. There isn't any music, but the dance is a kind of sprightly polka:

in pairs, they step right-left-right, and then back the other way, all in unison and in time, left-right-left, forward two paces and back one, and follow a couple of quick heel taps with a single toe tap before spinning about on the spot and giving a little jump to return to their original positions. And then begin again.

-6.

The bulk or heap—surprise, surprise—is not a bulk or heap, it's a flower. The man observing me, I can sense, thinks I must be a very stupid person. And nonetheless I am surprised, or I give the impression of surprise, who knows. The surprise comes not from inferring that I'm being watched, but at the sight of this large flower, which has no stem but lies flat on the stage, and on the central corolla of which, separated into five lobes, lies a woman, her head on a pillow-like fruit that gives off the smell of rotten flesh. A woman: she, too, wears a habit, but unlike those of the dancing nuns, hers is dazzling white and tight fitting, delineating the contours of her body. I move closer, and the nuns immediately stop their dancing. Their faces, so incredibly lined and wrinkled as almost to obscure the faces themselves, eyes included, put me in mind of those enormous tracts of land that would have existed before the continental drifts that formed the planet's current geography. They have gone past old age: they are old age itself. A timeframe apart. As though time had ceased to obey physical laws and was now little more than an accumulation, unnecessary, of dead skin. We've been expecting you, Jakarta, says the nun closest to me. They step to either side, forming a tunnel for me to pass through. Then I may admire her. So light and insubstantial—she reminds me of Clara. The scissors and a comb are in my hands, and there's a spray bottle tucked into my belt. But I am afraid to touch her. Afraid that as soon as I do, she will dissolve, or I will. I tell the ancient women that I can't. I'm sorry, I just don't have it in me. If I do this, I won't be able to go back. They all laugh. It's the only thing I have, the only thing, I try to say, but I can't seem to speak, and then there is a lock of the novice's hair in my left hand. Her hair is freezing cold; it hurts my fingers to touch it. I take some pincers and use them, separating the hair into three sections, making one central guide section that serves to establish left and right. Ice begins to crystallize on my fingertips. But the nuns aren't interested in that: they applaud each snip and fold as though it were a masterstroke, a true KO, another shovelful of earth on my own coffin. Soon my fingers are blue, strands of the novice's hair form a small black, frosty mound on the floor, and the smell of rotten meat coming from the flower begins to make me dizzy, but the old wrinkly bags go on clapping: the more cuts I make, the more they clap, and I realize I'm not in control, I'm powerless to stop, and the nuns form up and commence the dance again: right-left-right, hop, sidestep, and I snip-snip-snip more quickly, furiously, even, cutting in time to their dance, their heel taps and pauses and the recitation they begin to intersperse with their movements, the pungent ointments that bind their ghostly presences to the music in two-four time, and a long time passes in this way, I don't know how long, but the novice's hair seems never-ending, a never-ending abundance, seeming to grow thicker as I go on with my work, and I go on with my work, cutting, cutting, so the void seems to grow, a void anterior to everything, to the stage, to the patio, to all Jakarta, and I think these things as I go on cutting, cutting, not thinking of the hair I'm cutting but thinking of the void: Who shall claim it as their own? Where is it? Then I realize that the dance has stopped, the nuns have gathered around the flower, around us, and they have cutlery in their hands, old, rusty silverware. The cocoon is ready, says one, her voice metallic sounding (like Grandma's), and before I can make the final cut they fall hungrily on the body and begin to tear it to pieces. This, then, is what it is to need. A slight variation on fury. They tear off handfuls of her and stuff the handfuls in their mouths. And in spite of the great rends and gashes in her body, the novice doesn't bleed, though when one of the nuns raises a fork high and plunges it in, her eyes fly open. Eyes of stony black, thinks the man from his place in the room, while simultaneously becoming aware of a number of microscopic bugs that surge forward out of the flower and begin to feed on the scraps of flesh. The meat dropping from the maws of the nuns will serve to make new lives and new deaths, but my attention is focused almost entirely on the way the nuns ingest this fare, by the machines for ingesting they have become, even though their gums are bare of teeth.

-7.

The bulk or heap, as suspected, is neither. When the man lifts the silk sheet (a type of silk produced only by worms in neighboring Cambodia), a model of the city is revealed. A place he remembers being in. He recognizes the large body of water to one side of it, the abandoned sports stadium, the main square, the mill, the dockyards, the residential area. A place he has been to, but long ago—so long ago that, though he recognizes the intricately rendered buildings, it is beyond him to picture the people who lived in the city, what they are like in physical appearance. They are represented in the model by bedbugs that, though domesticated, scuttle away and hide at the sight of him. The city was part of an ancient civilization, he remembers, home to a people of singular rapaciousness that frequently teetered close to extinction. But the pet bedbugs have a relatively easy life. Just now, he can see them copulating inside the tiny houses. Not just copulating: putting on full pornographic spectacles, all manner of obscenities. I like the word *copulate*. It's a nicer way of saying *make them love you*. The buzzing noise in his head is intensifying. Buzzing, or maybe more like a smacking, or whips cracking . . . The bedbugs dance; they're using sex toys on one another, abusing one another in groups, no holds barred. The man wants to touch them. Play with them. But how clumsy he is, how big and clumsy: as he reaches down into the model city, the buildings immediately begin to topple to the ground.

-8.

No, it definitely, definitively, is neither bulk nor heap. It's a hazmat suit someone has dumped there, in the niche. It doesn't give off any smoke; the thinness of the air up here prevents combustion. What happened was this: as a last resort, with the snow piled many meters deep on top of him—both blocking his breathing apparatus and creating an excruciating downward pressure on his body—the man unstrapped his helmet, and, upon contact with the Jakartinese air, was instantly killed. Abnormal and very volatile levels of radon, argon, sulfur dioxide, helium, and neon make it impossible to breathe. The combination also creates extremely high winds, with masses of air tearing across the passes and valleys of the region at speeds of up to seventy-seven hundred kilometers per hour. Even at sea level, the atmospheric pressure in this strange country is impossible for the human body to withstand: the moment the helmet came off, within one billionth of a second, it made puree of the man's head.

-9.

The bulk or heap is not a bulk or heap. It's me. When finally the man lifts the silk sheet away, he then stands looking down for a long time. He opens his mouth, and I glimpse the forked tongue flickering inside. I look back at him, and I don't feel anything either.

-10.

The bulk or heap was a bulk or heap. The boys did not set fire to it on the final corner of summer. They did not shoot it full of bullets. They did not humiliate it. They did not beat it in the yard, at recess, on every day of every single year. They did not send it away to military

school. They used neither belts nor cables on it. It did not die from
infection. It just ceased to be.

-11.

The bulk or heap or mound or protuberance on the ground gives off
a foul stench. It is a pile of trash. Kovac, Morgan, and I stand over it.
We're suited up and are looking for something in the detritus. I don't
know what, but there seems to be some urgency about it. It doesn't
matter. We go on looking. The pile is enormous—extending as far
as the eye can see. We turn over anything at hand, picking up and
dropping empty packaging, strips of metal, cans, plastic bags, bits of
cloth, glass, wheel rims, jars, old urinals, dead dogs, dead children,
sections of hosepipe, food scraps, plastic bottles, fish scales, pencils,
charcoal, ash, newspapers, toilets, cardboard packaging—objects
that are good for nothing now except as landfill, as elements in these
new and autonomous territories. We are the founding fathers of the
mound. And its constituents too. Not even the Environment Agency
has jurisdiction in this new land. For all its fluidity and changeabil-
ity, we are its uncontested masters. And at the summit, the stench is
not quite so bad. I tell them this, but they ignore me. Up there, boys,
I say, up at the top. They don't want to know. But when Kovac sees me
start to wander off, he shouts, begins waving his hands around. I can
see his lopsided eyes through the visor. It's good to be with Kovac
again; it makes me happy, gives me a peaceful sensation—the peace
you experience only in memories. The peace of absence. How long
has it been since I was this close to him? I smile at him, feel sure he's
smiling, too, inside his helmet. Then, more calmly now, he tells me
to get back to work. Concentration, kid, he says: con-cen-tra-tion. So
I concentrate. Morgan's making the noise with his mouth. The noise
that annoys the shit out of me. Concentration, I mutter. But I don't
know what we're looking for. It could be anything. Sometimes it's
about looking but not trying to *find* anything, I tell myself, though

that seems more or less like class-A bullshit. And yet I go on, down on my knees, rummaging in the trash. I turn it over in my hands. I probe the slimy layers, sticky conjunction of sun and waste and percolating waters. Then I've got it; it's in my hand. Or rather, I see it— the eggplant purple of it—and then it's in my hand: a finger, a child's finger. But it's a finger all right, and fingers tend to come with hands; it's pretty unusual for them to go wandering about on their own. I clear away the nearby detritus, about ten feet around, and come up with the other four digits: the first one was the ring finger. Kovac and Morgan are busy pulling clear the body of a large, fat man—they keep dropping him—and haven't noticed my find. The Bug—it hits me: we've been wrong about it all along. How stupid we've been. We don't contract it, it isn't contagious. We're born with it. It reveals itself piecemeal, little by little, but then reaches a kind of critical mass, becoming suddenly apparent to a large group of people. Now, two things happen—many things happen, but two stand out: the clicking of Morgan's tongue grows louder, and he starts doing it faster, and the ring finger, to all appearances quite solid, turns out to have the same consistency as gelatin. These two sensations, allied with the smell of putrefaction, are in perfect harmony with our digging efforts. And I must say there is something pleasant about the pliable, spongy consistency of the ring finger. I give it a little squeeze, testing its firmness, only for it to pop between my own fingers like a puss-filled zit. Oh: no more finger. I decide to pull out the rest of the body, and this time to be a bit more careful. First I come up with the other hand, the left one, then the right forearm; when I pull on the arm, it comes away from the submerged body at the shoulder. So I put the arm to one side; I'll get the rest out and then piece it all together again. A thousand times I must have done this, it's like a muscle memory now: which bones go with which, which expanses of flesh and which organs you need to be most careful with. I could assemble a body for you like a wardrobe or a chest of drawers from a box. But, like the rest of the objects that comprise the towering mound, the child's body parts aren't a child's body parts anymore: they have become part of *us,* even if I couldn't say precisely how. I find the head a little way off, in a shopping bag. Birdface's head has no useful function either anymore; it's trash like everything else here, there's a cut on the forehead, and a beret's been sewn into the nape of the neck with black thread. I hear two heavy thuds, and the ground shakes. An earthquake, I think. Morgan's tongue-clicking stops, and there's the sound of another object, a large bulky mass, striking the trash heap. I turn and see that Kovac has been half swallowed by the heap. And Morgan has an enormous stone in his arms, I see, shiny and very dark. He's breathing heavily inside the suit, and Kovac, sinking down, almost entirely subsumed by the heap, can hardly move. It's me next: when he's finished Kovac off, he's going to come for me. But there isn't space inside the helmet for Kovac's tongue. There's no way for his tongue—very long, and moving independently of the rest of his body—to wriggle out of the helmet, no way for it to get free and wrap around his neck. I watch as he gradually begins to turn purple, the same purple as Helguera's body, becoming shapeless, too, the bones seemingly suddenly removed, the sinews and tendons, all bodily tissue. I can't find his original shape, but that doesn't matter either now. Nobody's coming to claim him now. Somewhere a dog howls. I go back with the dogs: to the time before howls. Morgan wants to come. He knows his place: every two or three decades, it manifests. And it can manifest in such a variety of different ways: hence why in these lands the people have never fully been able to deal with it. Morgan, Morgan, Morgan. With his last remaining ounce of strength he raises the stone high and brings it down on Kovac's head. That's all he's got, nothing left now: he totters for a moment, stumbles, and falls. Gasping, he tries to get up. Another tremor shakes the trash heap, knocking him down once more. Then he turns toward me and begins dragging himself in my direction, stone under one arm. Was it the same in the tunnel? Did he try to finish me off down there too? But yes, here you can see the sky. Endless grays. Kovac gives a final shudder. The howling has grown louder, there's more than one dog now, though I still can't see them anywhere. Morgan,

Morgan, Morgan. How can such skinny arms be so strong? He drags himself along, a trail of blood in his wake. How slow he is. I could get up and run off in the time it's going to take him to get to me. And if it weren't for the fact I'm already very far away. Not ahead of him, or behind. Just far.

LITERATURE
is not the same thing as
PUBLISHING

Coffee House Press began as a small letterpress operation in 1972 and has grown into an internationally renowned nonprofit publisher of literary fiction, essay, poetry, and other work that doesn't fit neatly into genre categories.

Coffee House is both a publisher and an arts organization. Through our *Books in Action* program and publications, we've become interdisciplinary collaborators and incubators for new work and audience experiences. Our vision for the future is one where a publisher is a catalyst and connector.

Funder Acknowledgments

Coffee House Press is an internationally renowned independent book publisher and arts nonprofit based in Minneapolis, MN; through its literary publications and *Books in Action* program, Coffee House acts as a catalyst and connector—between authors and readers, ideas and resources, creativity and community, inspiration and action.

Coffee House Press books are made possible through the generous support of grants and donations from corporations, state and federal grant programs, family foundations, and the many individuals who believe in the transformational power of literature. This activity is made possible by the voters of Minnesota through a Minnesota State Arts Board Operating Support grant, thanks to the legislative appropriation from the Arts and Cultural Heritage Fund. Coffee House also receives major operating support from the Amazon Literary Partnership, Jerome Foundation, McKnight Foundation, Target Foundation, and the National Endowment for the Arts (NEA). To find out more about how NEA grants impact individuals and communities, visit www.arts.gov.

Coffee House Press receives additional support from the Elmer L. & Eleanor J. Andersen Foundation; the David & Mary Anderson Family Foundation; Bookmobile; Dorsey & Whitney LLP; Foundation Technologies; Fredrikson & Byron, P.A.; the Fringe Foundation; Kenneth Koch Literary Estate; the Matching Grant Program Fund of the Minneapolis Foundation; Mr. Pancks' Fund in memory of Graham Kimpton; the Schwab Charitable Fund; Schwegman, Lundberg & Woessner, P.A.; the Silicon Valley Community Foundation; and the U.S. Bank Foundation.

The Publisher's Circle of Coffee House Press

Publisher's Circle members make significant contributions to Coffee House Press's annual giving campaign. Understanding that a strong financial base is necessary for the press to meet the challenges and opportunities that arise each year, this group plays a crucial part in the success of Coffee House's mission.

Recent Publisher's Circle members include many anonymous donors, Suzanne Allen, Patricia A. Beithon, the E. Thomas Binger & Rebecca Rand Fund of the Minneapolis Foundation, Andrew Brantingham, Robert & Gail Buuck, Dave & Kelli Cloutier, Louise Copeland, Jane Dalrymple-Hollo & Stephen Parlato, Mary Ebert & Paul Stembler, Kaywin Feldman & Jim Lutz, Chris Fischbach & Katie Dublinski, Sally French, Jocelyn Hale & Glenn Miller, the Rehael Fund-Roger Hale/ Nor Hall of the Minneapolis Foundation, Randy Hartten & Ron Lotz, Dylan Hicks & Nina Hale, William Hardacker, Randall Heath, Jeffrey Hom, Carl & Heidi Horsch, the Amy L. Hubbard & Geoffrey J. Kehoe Fund, Kenneth & Susan Kahn, Stephen & Isabel Keating, Julia Klein, the Kenneth Koch Literary Estate, Cinda Kornblum, Jennifer Kwon Dobbs & Stefan Liess, the Lambert Family Foundation, the Lenfestey Family Foundation, Joy Linsday Crow, Sarah Lutman & Rob Rudolph, the Carol & Aaron Mack Charitable Fund of the Minneapolis Foundation, George & Olga Mack, Joshua Mack & Ron Warren, Gillian McCain, Malcolm S. McDermid & Katie Windle, Mary & Malcolm McDermid, Sjur Midness & Briar Andresen, Maureen Millea Smith & Daniel Smith, Peter Nelson & Jennifer Swenson, Enrique & Jennifer Olivarez, Alan Polsky, Marc Porter & James Hennessy, Robin Preble, Alexis Scott, Ruth Stricker Dayton, Jeffrey Sugerman & Sarah Schultz, Nan G. & Stephen C. Swid, Kenneth Thorp in memory of Allan Kornblum & Rochelle Ratner, Patricia Tilton, Joanne Von Blon, Stu Wilson & Melissa Barker, Warren D. Woessner & Iris C. Freeman, and Margaret Wurtele.

For more information about the Publisher's Circle and other ways to support Coffee House Press books, authors, and activities, please visit www.coffeehousepress.org/pages/support or contact us at info@coffeehousepress.org.

RODRIGO MÁRQUEZ TIZANO (Mexico City, 1984) is a writer and editor. He has been the editor in chief of *VICE* magazine in Mexico and Argentina and is a founding editor of La Dulce Ciencia Ediciones, a publishing imprint dedicated to the world of boxing. He received his MFA from NYU and is completing a PhD at Cornell University. *Jakarta* is his first novel.

THOMAS BUNSTEAD has translated some of the leading Spanish-language writers working today, most recently *Optic Nerve* by María Gainza and *The Nocilla Trilogy* by Agustín Fernández Mallo. His own writing has appeared in publications such as the *Paris Review Daily*, the *Times Literary Supplement*, and the *White Review*. He is an editor at the literary translation journal *In Other Words*.

Jakarta was designed by
Bookmobile Design & Digital Publisher Services.
Text is set in Arno Pro.